SEASONS OF FLIGHT

~

Dealing sensitively with the dilemmas faced by immigrants who find themselves at home neither in their land of origin nor in their adopted country, Thapa avoids the temptation to make larger political or social statements about the two societies [...] Thapa's lucid prose describing [her protagonist's] thoughts and emotions rings true to life, and is the novel's most significant strength [...] [A] near-perfect performance.'—*Himal Southasian*

'As one woman's personal story, as an immigrant narrative, Thapa's novel is engaging. But it's the background of Nepali politics and the country's moment in history that lends it force. After all, it is a territory where Thapa, whose former work includes the critically acclaimed *Forget Kathmandu*, is on firm ground.'—*The Indian Express*

'A brilliantly poetic and yet so contemporary a tale of a young Nepali woman's [...] journey in search of personal fulfillment [...] Through all [the] multiple layers and themes [...] [y]ou sense Nepal's melancholy and feel the emptiness of life torn by strife, and you also live the air-conditioned loneliness of Los Angeles. And this is the mark of an extraordinary author.'—*The Sunday Indian*

~

By the same author:

FICTION

Tilled Earth: Stories

The Tutor of History

NON-FICTION

A Boy from Siklis: The Life and Times of Chandra Gurung

Forget Kathmandu: An Elegy for Democracy

Mustang Bhot in Fragments

The Lives We Have Lost: Essays and Opinions on Nepal

Seasons of Flight

MANJUSHREE THAPA

ALEPH

ALEPH

ALEPH BOOK COMPANY
An independent publishing firm
promoted by ***Rupa Publications India***

Published in 2012 by
Aleph Book Company
7/16 Ansari Road, Daryaganj
New Delhi 110002

First published in India by Penguin Books India 2010

ISBN: 978-93-822774-9-1

1 3 5 7 9 10 8 6 4 2

For sale in the Indian subcontinent only.

Typeset in Adobe Garamond Pro by SÜRYA, New Delhi

Printed by Replika Press Pvt. Ltd
Kundli, Haryana

To Daniel:
Being in the world

Sire, I am from the other country.
—Ivan Chtcheglov
Formulary for a New Urbanism

The way back is lost, the one obsession.
The worst is over.
The worst is yet to come.
—Carolyn Forché
The Testimony of Light

Those who dwell, as scientists or laymen, among the beauties and mysteries of the earth are never alone or weary of life.
—Rachel Carson
A Sense of Wonder

What do I really know about love? I have had some experience, and feel fluent enough for my own satisfaction. Love, I find is like singing. Everybody can do enough to satisfy themselves, though it may not impress the neighbors as being very much.
—Zora Neale Hurston
Dust Tracks on a Road

Contents

~

~

Being Nepali

~

An American woman, a schoolteacher, earnest and frizzy, once came up to Prema and asked, 'Mind if I ask where you're from? Originally, I mean?' But when she heard the answer she just stammered, unable, perhaps, to admit that she didn't know where that was.

Most Americans did better. They would say, 'Oh' or, 'Wow' or even, 'Cool' and nod in a friendly manner. Sometimes Prema would help them out by adding, 'It is near India,' or 'Where Mount Everest is,' or 'You have heard of the Sherpas?' so that they might say, 'Geez, that's real far,' or 'I could have sworn you were Mexican/Italian/Spanish,' or 'You speak very good English.' And then she would smile: 'Thank you.'

Every now and then, though, a response would stop her. One day, a woman on the bus heard her say Nippon and expressed her disgust at the practice of eating raw fish: 'That's like eating you-know-what!' she exclaimed. Another man, a dark-skinned grocer, South Asian himself, baffled her with, 'Aren't you usually from Pakistan?' It was Prema's turn to stammer. She had also learnt that to the foreign ear, the country's name could sound like 'nipple'. More commonly, though, what Americans heard was Naples, as in: 'I just love pasta,' or, 'My husband and I went to Rome for our honeymoon, but we never made it to Naples.'

'Where are you from?'

If possible Prema dodged the truth: 'Pasadena.' 'Compton.' 'San Pedro.' Sometimes she would say, 'I am from India,' because Americans had at least heard of India. She envied Indians this. And the conversations that followed could be unexpected to her: 'I was just speaking to a man in India about my credit card!' Though lying did sometimes land her in trouble. Once, downtown by the skyscrapers, she got talking to a security guard of a bank building, and when she said she was Indian he said, 'Me too,' and asked, 'Which tribe?' Unable to explain herself, she retracted: 'I am from the state of Indiana, actually.' 'Geez,' he said. 'That's real far.'

It was and it was not far, where she came from. Some days her birth village felt centuries away, and other days it was too close; she could not get far enough away from it. Her family home—which she still thought of as hers, though she had not lived in it since she was seventeen—was sturdy, two-storeyed, of stone. It had felt sheltering, and safe, when she used to run through the bamboo grove past the Shiva-Parvati temple that bordered the terraced rice fields, to school. Only later, when she had left the village to go to high school, then college, in the capital, Kathmandu, had she discovered that her family had been poor. The house, the grove, the temple and the terraced fields were perched at the foothills of the eastern himals. A silver mist rolled in all year. Prema had shivered through all her childhood.

She lived, now, in America, in a spare, uncluttered flat with a transient feel. Her only memento from home was an ammonite, a lustrous stone the colour of shale, the shape of a lopsided egg. A fossil of marine life from when the himals were below the sea, millennia ago. Where a granite band ran through it, its halves opened with a clack to reveal a coiled impression of an exoskeleton.

The ammonite had belonged to her mother. A Hindu ascetic who came wandering through Prema's birth village had given it to her. Her mother, devout, used to worship the coil at the centre as a shaligram, an avatar of Bishnu. She kept it in her bedroom shrine, and every morning sprinkled rice grains on it and made offerings of flowers and vermilion powder. Praying for what? The ammonite sat at the centre of the shrine, with pictures of the deities—Krishna, Parvati, Shiva, Laksmi—placed lovingly around it.

Centuries away. Not far enough.

Prema had wanted to reinvent herself in America, but—What is there to being human? The body which desires, persistent and unreasonable; thoughts and temperaments. Instincts. A capacity to harm. And history, which lingers as a spectre.

Los Angeles. In the mornings she took the No. 232 bus north, transferring first to the No. 444, then to the No. 442 to a non-profit by an exit ramp. In the evenings she retraced her way back along the bus routes, sitting among Americans—a mother with three children of differing skin tones, a man carrying four briefcases, a man with fuzzy pink headphones: 'And how's baby Rose?' '¿Es abrir?' 'You gotta keep at it.' '¡A mi me lo vas a contra!' If she was not going out for dinner, she would cook a meal of daal, or a fenugreek-eggplant, or cumin-cauliflower, or close approximations with the ingredients at hand. Sometimes, after dinner, she would look out the window through a pair of binoculars that she had bought upon graduating from college: a 10x50 that offered a clear, steady view on to the world. The houses on her street were joined in pairs. Duplexes, the Americans called them. Wood shingles, stucco, tile. In the night-time—the electroluminescence—mica sparkled dimly on the road, eerie and other-worldly. Every now and then she still wondered what she was doing in America. There was a bluegum eucalyptus across the way, its lanceolet leaves a velvety, shimmering green. An Australian import. Often by its bark Prema caught the sweep of a butterfly on a winding flight path. Or she saw a darting: a squirrel or a raccoon, or a rat come to forage for garbage. She took in the concrete of the pavements, the metal grates of the manhole covers. Prema was not gifted at introspection. It was through the examination of the external world that she glimpsed what lay within.

She had taken the ammonite from her mother's shrine when she had left home at seventeen. She had held on to it through college and kept it with her, a talisman, when—upon studying forestry—she went to work in a hill bazaar on the far side of the country. By then the war had come to her birth village. The Maoist rebels had come one day, recruiting one member from each family. From Prema's family they had taken her sixteen-year-old sister Bijaya. Her father had feared a similar fate for Prema. Month after month, when she had telephoned home, her father had advised her not to visit. Years passed. She did not go back.

Now here she was. Out the window, above the street, at a horizon line marked by high-tension wires and palm trees: a lurid city sky, the darkness banished by pink fading to purple to charcoal and ash.

'Where are you from?'

Why did Americans ask this when they were so unprepared for the reply?

'Where are you from?'

'Nepal.'

Happy Family in Mongolia

~

The wounds of childhood, relics around which deposits have hardened, adamantine. Prema had known early of the world's sorrows. She had been eight when her mother had given birth to a baby, a baby who, unlike the ones before, had come warm and pulsing into life. A sister! Her parents had named the baby Bijaya: Victory. All that week, Prema had skipped the game of marbles that she used to play after school, running home in excitement to fuss over her sister. Her mother had complained of the cold, shivering despite the blankets her father drew over her and the coal fires he lit by the bedside. At night her tremors rattled the bed. One morning she lost consciousness. When Prema returned from school that afternoon, she saw that the neighbours had gathered outside. Inside, her aunt—her mother's sister—was nursing her sister. Prema rushed to her mother's bedside. It took her a while to understand why it was vacant. Her father had already taken her mother to the riverside for the cremation. Prema had been oblivious of her dying.

Her mother's loss ended her childhood. Their father had been an energetic man once, full of plans; but his ambitions now moved like phantoms in the empty spaces of the family home. All he wanted was a better life for his daughters. As soon as Prema completed high school, she applied herself, at her father's urging, to progressing—going away to college, studying forestry, and eventually landing a job. There had been no set direction in her movements. She had taken the best opportunities available, following a zigzag trail of chance and happenstance.

That trail had led her to a hill bazaar straight across the country, a bazaar only slightly better off than her birth village. There was no trace of government here. She was hired by a non-government organization that did a bit of everything. The organization constructed irrigation canals and culverts to boost the yield of the bazaar-dwellers' terraced fields. It gave interest-free loans to the poor so that they could rear chickens and goats. It brought health workers in to run health camps and vaccination drives. It ran non-formal education classes so that grown men and women could learn to read and write. Development, all this was called. The bazaar-dwellers were grateful for the work and treated the staff as family.

Prema worked alongside a senior forester, Trailokya, to offset the carbon footprint of a British corporation. The conservation programme subsidized fuel-efficient stoves so that the bazaar-dwellers would use less firewood for cooking. It opened kerosene depots to provide an alternative source of fuel. It started plantations to meet local timber needs. In monthly meetings, Trailokya and Prema urged the bazaar-dwellers to set limits to the forest resources they used. They did what they could, and they did it in good faith, believing that every little thing helped; but sometimes Prema felt that they were coaxing the poor, who already consumed so little, to consume even less.

Still, the job paid well. She had studied forestry expressly because it could lead to a well-paying job. As college had drawn to an end, Prema's friends had hatched elaborate schemes to migrate to India, or farther, to Australia, Europe, Canada, America. There was so little in Nepal, everyone just wanted to leave. And also, for those who felt they were from a shabby Third World country, it was hard not to believe that life in a richer land was more—proper, solid. At a certain age Prema had also wondered whether she shouldn't go abroad, but then she had got this job and settled into the hill bazaar.

Yet, one day, she entered her name in the American green-card lottery. It was late in the season of winds, the season of restlessness, when the breezes shook the last of the dead leaves off the trees, denuding the branches. That morning Trailokya and Prema went to the tree plantation outside the bazaar to measure the progress of the new saplings. On the way back Prema lost her balance and slipped, landing in a water-logged gully. Her clothes got soaked. Trailokya suggested they stop by a teashop to dry up.

The matron who ran the teashop clucked when she saw Prema's clothes. 'Tch, tch, tch, you must be freezing, Bahini!' She poured them two steaming hot glasses of black-pepper tea, then turned to the men at the next table, hunched over a tatty chessboard: 'Oh boys, are you going to spend the whole day playing games?'

'Ah, it's your tea, Didi, it keeps us wanting more.'

'Any excuse!' She refilled their glasses.

Outside, the wind swept through the land with a low keening. Beyond the teashop window, across the way, Kanchha, the fourteen-year-old son of a retired Gurkha soldier, was hammering a banner above the bazaar's telephone booth and cybercafe, lodged in his father's house. The wind kept whipping the banner out of his hands. When at last the boy fixed it in place, he moved back to inspect his handiwork. Straining against the wind, the banner announced: ATOMATIC GARANTEE GREEN CARD.

'What automatic guarantees are you promising, eh, Kanchha?' Trailokya called out to the boy.

'Which ones do you want, Sir?' Kanchha called back.

'Lots of money so I can keep my wife happy!' Trailokya said.

In the teashop the chess players guffawed.

'There's lots of money in America,' Kanchha replied. 'The deadline for the green-card lottery is coming!'

'And what would I do in America, boy?'

'You could make money saving Americané trees!'

Trailokya laughed; but Kanchha was in earnest. He came over to the teashop window, focusing on Trailokya. 'It's only two hundred rupees, Sir. I'll fill out the form myself.'

Trailokya had married late. He and his wife had just had their first son. Perhaps he dreamed, if idly, of going abroad one day, getting rich. 'My old lady can go?' he asked. 'What about my son? Can he go too?'

'It's an automatic guarantee!'

'La ta.' Trailokya shrugged affably. 'Who knows? Maybe it'll open up the boy's fortunes.'

Kanchha immediately turned to Prema: 'Sister, you must also apply.'

'What would I do in America?' she said. But—so winning was Kanchha—she went along.

There was not much to the application. After Trailokya fetched his wife and baby, Kanchha led them into his father's cybercafe, a village room partitioned by glass-and-plywood walls into four booths. In one booth three schoolboys were ogling a screen showing a bare-breasted blonde, her thighs splayed for exposure. They quickly blocked the screen as the others passed by. Kanchha led them to the back of the room and made them stand, one by one, in front of a whitewashed wall so that he could take their photographs. Within minutes he had downloaded the photographs on to a computer and filled out the forms online. On everyone's form he listed the address and telephone number of the cybercafe. At the end he handed out receipts. 'Done.'

'Two hundred rupees for that?' Trailokya feigned horror.

'What's two hundred rupees for a rich sir like you?' Kanchha said. 'You'd spend that much on a single plate of momos in America!'

Prema laughed. 'You can't find momos in America.'

Kanchha grinned. 'Yes, you can, Sister—but they'd be made of cow's meat!'

It was dark by the time Trailokya and his family headed back to their lodgings and Prema to hers. She rented a room in the house of a schoolteacher couple who were, as they said about themselves, progressive. Yet their progressiveness had its limits. They were occupied in those days with preparations for the wedding of their daughter, a docile eighteen-year-old who had been under pressure to marry since passing out of high school. Her parents had found her a suitable groom, a same-caste engineer with employment in the capital, and prospects of going abroad. The astrologers had set the wedding date. Relatives from nearby villages were always visiting, and the house rang with cheer.

'Did you feel the tremors, Bahini?' the schoolteacher wife called out from amid a circle of aunts when Prema got home that evening. 'The whole house shook! Just a few hours ago. Did you feel it?'

An earthquake? 'I missed it,' Prema said.

'We all ran out of the house, screaming! This one'—she cuffed a younger aunt—'left her baby in the house and ran out!'

Everyone burst out laughing. Prema smiled, and with a polite nod to the aunts, excused herself.

Dinner was always served late in that house. Upstairs, in her room, Prema opened the windows and scanned the inky-blue hills. The himals were not visible from the bazaar, but their foothills ringed the north. She picked up her binoculars and traced the hills up to the ridge, where—according to bazaar gossip—a troop of Maoist rebels was camped. There was no movement on the ridge. There seemed to be no movement at all in the universe. On the surface everything was still. Beneath, though, the tectonic plates were pushing against each other, causing the land to churn and the soil to shift, setting off earthquakes, folding and buckling the land into hills and mountains, adding inches to the himals every year. The thin crust of human habitation—the hill bazaar—could be swept away in one convulsion.

Prema felt a shivering in the marrow. Shuttering the window, she turned on the radio and sat on the bed, drawing the blankets around her for warmth. The local news was on. A road had been built in a remote district, eye camps had been held in another district, agricultural experts in the nation's capital had discovered a planting technique that doubled the yield of rice. On the bedside table, beside her mother's ammonite, lay a stack of days-old newspapers. She picked up one and read about an accident that had occurred on a mountain highway. Two clashes between the Maoists and the army had claimed fourteen lives. A curfew had been imposed in a border town…

That was Prema's life in Nepal. There was nothing really wrong with it. Though the country was at war, she was safe. Had it been in her power, she would have changed a few things, of course. She might have lived in a town rather than in a bazaar, a town large enough to have a cinema, and shops, and restaurants of the kind she and her friends used to go to in college. She might have had more like-minded friends for company. She might have been more—free. And— Her ageing father did assure her that he was all right in the village, but she might have visited her birth village now and again, just to make sure.

It was for her sister Bijaya, more than for herself, that Prema wished a different life. She wished she could do something about the lack of prospects, the lack of a future with which Bijaya had come into this world, motherless. Bijaya had grown into a mulish girl occupied only with chores and errands, taciturn and closed-off, even to their father, even to Prema. Perhaps she felt that her birth had destroyed her family. She had not passed out of high school despite their father's exhortations: 'You must progress.' When the Maoist rebels came by the village, they had had to force others to join them. Not Bijaya. 'She went just like that,' their father had told Prema afterwards, on the telephone. He had sounded bewildered. She had left the village as a new recruit. Had she really seen a future in warfare? The idiot girl. Now and then word filtered back to their father that she was still alive, she was well; but no one knew, any more, where she was or what she was doing.

Prema was the one who had left, she was the one who had progressed. She telephoned her father every month; and her organization's head office, in the capital, deposited a share of her salary directly into his bank account. 'You are as good as a son to me,' was how her father expressed his pride in her. Yet she knew that he considered her life incomplete, as she was not married. He did not know about Rajan.

Rajan lived and worked in a village a two hours' walk up from the hill bazaar. He headed the non-government organization's poverty-alleviation programme. Every few weeks he would come by the bazaar, and he and Prema would walk together to the town at the base of the hills and spend a night, or sometimes two nights, there. In their traditional milieu they kept their attachment a secret. In the hill bazaar Prema led a staid spinster's life. She did feel an emptiness in the evenings, but she tried to be content. She read. She listened to the news. After the local news came the national, then the international news. The newspapers and the radio kept Prema connected—or feeling connected—to the world.

That evening, the newspaper photographs were spotty with low-grade ink. One was of a Hindu guru in India who had been charged with conspiracy to murder: he had hired a hit man to kill a rival guru. Another photograph was of a family at a dining table, gathered around a large bowl. There was steam rising off a bowl, a bowl full of...dumplings. Momos. Examining the photograph, Prema's mouth suddenly watered; she felt a tingling for hot, juicy dumplings savoury with onions, cumin and coriander. The caption underneath the photograph read: *Happy Family in Mongolia.*

'You must be hungry, Prema-didi.' The daughter of the

house—who was soon to be married—came in carrying a plate of daal-bhat.

'Not at all,' Prema said for decorum's sake.

She ate at the desk as the daughter stood idling.

Afterwards, Prema lay in bed listening to the BBC national service, then to the world news. The British prime minister had said something controversial that day. An oil agreement had been signed in Venezuela. The United Nations had voiced concern over Haiti. A group of lawyers was challenging Guantanámo Bay. There had been unrest in Hungary, South Korea, Bolivia… At one point Prema heard a familiar plop at the foot of her bed. A dung beetle had dropped from the ceiling.

The Woman Who Was Drifting

~

Three years later she was working as a homecare attendant for an old lady, Esther King, who lived in a beachside neighbourhood in Los Angeles. Prema herself lived inland on a dry, grassy hill, sharing a rickety house with two young women. Housemates. To reach Esther's house each morning, she had to catch the No. 2 on a dishevelled boulevard near the hill. Then, downtown by the skyscrapers, she had to transfer to the No. 33, which coursed an avenue of small businesses: Computer Systems and Coin Laundry, a neon NAILS sign, a red shop named Carniceria. Date palms swaying in the breeze. At an underpass she had to switch buses again, this time to the No. 220, which went past tranquil residential blocks to the coast.

Esther's house was on a bluff by the ocean, just across from a chain-link fence demarcating the boundary of the international airport, LAX, where Prema had landed two-and-a-half years ago. Airplanes roared overhead all day. The house looked small from the outside, but inside it was plush, and crammed full of fine objects. There were photographs on the hallway walls—a boy on a felucca, a skyline with minarets—and carpets on the floor. The living room was crowded with sofa sets all upholstered in silk, and decorative tables of gilt wood, hardwood, carved teak. The bookshelves were lined with goblets, baskets, figurines, shells. An oil painting hung above the mantle, a cobalt-blue woman with a blank expression. Esther had painted the cobalt-blue woman herself. There was a studio room full of other paintings by her: women in red, green, yellow, all with blank expressions. The dining-room wall was decorated with abstract paintings. All the closets were jammed with appliances: vacuum cleaners, humidifiers, dust-busters, air-purifiers, irons, ironing boards. Even the bathrooms were crowded, with watercolours on the walls, and on the sink counters potpourri, handmade soaps, candles that had never been lit, pastel-coloured tissue boxes, hand towels and creams scented with essence of peppermint, wild rose, hemp, bergamot, Meyer lemon.

Esther's granddaughter Natalie—a lawyer in a perpetual hurry—had hired Prema after the briefest of interviews, with only the most glancing warning: 'Nana isn't quite— The symptoms are just beginning to show. Do you know much about dementia?'

She had tacked a list of instructions on the kitchen corkboard: a list of DOs, DONTs and NEVERs. Some days Natalie also left a shopping list—milk, orange juice, eggs—and a few dollar bills. *This note is legal tender.* She also left recipes on the corkboard, and her various telephone numbers, and emergency numbers—the police department, the fire department, the ambulance—as well as numbers for people Prema never met: a Randy Miller and a Jen Rustig, a Morgan Hausman, a Jay Kleeberg, a Ron Singer, a Beth Martis, a Daniel Brenson. Americans.

Following instructions, Prema would feed Esther's cat every morning as the jet-black Bengal brushed against her legs, purring.

Then she would check in on Esther. In her room, the old lady would be sitting up in her gilt-frame bed. 'Good morning, dear. Can you help me get to the little girl's room?'

After Esther was done with her toilet, Prema would help her into one of the fine, finicky dresses she liked to wear, allowing her to fuss awhile in front of a full-length mirror—'Something's chafing. Can you redo the belt, dear? The buttons go like this. That's right.' Prema would brush and set her hair and help her put on cream, perfume, lipstick. Esther was very particular about her grooming. When she was ready, she ate breakfast in the dining room, babbling: 'That green house on the other side of the bluff? Abbot Kinney camped there. Make sure the yogurt is fresh, dear.' She was upbeat by temperament, but there was, apparently, no directing her mind. She would switch from topic to topic without warning: 'Papayas may be full of vitamins but they taste rotten. If Doctor Ismaili weren't so dashing I wouldn't listen to a thing he says... Did the delivery boy bring in the papers? Read me the headlines! What is your name?'

'Prema.'

'Prema, the butterflies are out there.'

After breakfast Esther would watch television for a few hours: Americans confessing their dark secrets to talk-show hosts. Most days she would want to have lunch on the beach. Prema would have to kit her with sunblock lotion, sunglasses, a sun hat, a windcheater and blankets before steering her wheelchair along the LAX chain-link fence. On the sand, she would help Esther to a bench by a dune overrun by mallows and ice plants. They would have sandwiches looking at the ocean, a million glitters of light.

Prema had never been to the ocean before this; she had been

caught up inland. The beach here was not attractive. Airplanes were constantly landing at or taking off from LAX—one at a time, two at a time. An industrial-water treatment plant loomed nearby, its stacks spewing fumes. A drainpipe lay at the centre of the beach, gushing muddy liquids—waste water?—into the ocean. Nevertheless, Americans lay on the sand, tanning their fit, toned bodies. Rollerbladers whipped by on a bicycle path, people spun frisbees and lunged after volleyballs. Some afternoons, two bikini-clad teenagers, a blonde and a brunette, would practise gymnastics by the dunes. The blonde would do a backflip, then the brunette would imitate her. For a while they would discuss what they had done. Then they would do it all over again.

A friend of Esther's, an old man, usually joined them on the beach, a beer-filled coffee cup in hand and in the other, something he had found beachcombing: 'Esther, doll. A present.'

'Oh, Sam! A limpet!'

The two of them would talk, not always with each other:

'I missed you, doll.' 'Sam, do you remember the ambassador's daughter?' 'Would have visited you at home, but I joined a seniors' chi gong class.' 'She caused quite a scandal!' 'The instructor's this skinny girl, always saying let the chi flow.' 'A Moslem! I believe her parents sent her back.' 'The crane pose my ass, if you'll pardon my—' 'A pity, such a spirited girl.' 'That's why I couldn't visit you, doll.'

Afterwards Prema would take Esther home, bathe her, and put her, soft and warm, into bed, where she would read novels—large-print romances loaned from a library by a boat harbour, not far away. During this lull Prema would bicycle to the library, or to a nearby grocery store called the Home Mart, except the M had come loose, and was dangling upside down. Home Wart. At five she would prepare Esther's dinner, and by six she would have her dressed in a bathrobe and bedroom slippers, eating in the dining room as the television news blared: the city council had approved a storm-water treatment facility, the mayor had pledged money for affordable housing…'The Brookners on Redlands have lovely children!' Esther would babble over the news. 'The eldest is a railway engineer in Corona del Mar. All the girls used to swoon over the youngest. A psychiatrist in Manhattan. I don't remember what the girl does. She's a— I was hoping our Theo would marry her, but Mary snapped him up!'

Natalie would burst into the house at six-thirty and slam into her room upstairs. When the advertisements came on television—ask your doctor about this new drug—Prema would get up to leave.

'Bye, Esther.'

And the old lady would startle. 'What's happening?' she would cry.

'I will see you tomorrow.'

'What's happening?'

'I will come again tomorrow, Esther.'

'Ah.' Esther would eventually compose herself. 'Goodnight, dear.'

From what Prema could piece together, Esther's life had once been quite charmed. After hearing Esther talk for days about her husband Tim and shells, Prema realized that he had worked for the oil company, Shell. He had been posted abroad for many years, though Prema could not tell where. She learned that the hallway photograph of the boy on the felucca was from Alexandria, Egypt. The skyline with minarets was from Tangier, Morocco. The crystal goblets on the living-room shelves were from Romania, and the wicker baskets from the Philippines. Prema could not tell whether Esther had actually been to these places. 'I always dreamed of visiting the man-made islands of Titicaca,' the old lady would say one minute, and the next minute she would be lecturing Prema on the uses of rabbit-skin glue.

It was little use trying to find out more. One morning, Prema pointed at the painting above the mantle, of the cobalt-blue woman. 'You painted that woman, Esther?' She did not like the woman's blank expression, but she said, 'She is a pretty woman.'

'Not a woman, dear. Just: woman. And those'—Esther pointed at the abstract paintings on the dining-room wall—'are dreamings, the habitats of anteaters, kangaroos and armadillos, from Australia.'

'You have been to Australia, Esther?'

'All the furniture is antique, mind. We shipped the dining table from Spain, and commissioned a furniture-maker in Palo Alto to design matching chairs. Have you seen the tea cosy, dear? The one we got in Belize?'

Prema did not know what a tea cosy was.

'There used to be a pavilion, but it burned down. Back when all this'—Esther flipped her hand—'was a lagoon.'

Esther's husband Tim had died long ago—of what cause Prema never learned. Her stepson Theo, who was Natalie's father—was Tim's son from a previous marriage. He was a stockbroker across the country, in the state of New Jersey. His wife Mary telephoned Esther once a week. Every few days a neighbour, Elizabeth Beard, came by and gossiped about the goings-on at the church where her husband served as pastor. There was beer-happy Sam, at the beach. Once a week, a Colombian woman named Mercury would come to clean the house. She worked fast, hardly pausing for breath, and left the rooms smelling of spray-can juniper. A gardener named Romiro came twice a week. At the end of the day he would come in to chat briefly, in Spanish, with Esther. That was it. Prema never met any of the people whose names were up on the kitchen corkboard. Most days it was just Esther and her.

At the end of the day, Prema would take the bus inland to the dry, grassy hill, to a street of one-storey houses with abandoned lawns and lonely front porches. All the buildings on the street were rickety. Her house was toothpaste-green, with iron grills at the windows and three latches on the front door. One of her housemates, Meg Williams, managed the house for the landlord, a man named Henry Little whom Prema never met. She had to mail him a cheque at the beginning of each month. Meg was big-boned, with a dark-chocolate complexion and glossy black eyes, the first black—African American—person Prema knew. She was garrulous to the point of compulsiveness. Whenever Prema came across her—in the kitchen, preparing dinner, or in the common room, watching television—Meg would say, 'Heya,' and say something else, then continue non-stop, as though Prema had asked her a series of questions that she needed, urgently, to answer. Prema learned, in this manner, that Meg had once been in retail, but now was a nursing student at a college that she called the Keck. She had grown up in a place called Greenville, which Prema later discovered was in the state of South Carolina. Her father, Frank, used to be an electrician, but was now retired. Her mother, Ginny, wanted to move to a condo in a place called Miami, in the state of Florida; but her father was happy in Greenville, and Meg was glad she could still visit her childhood home. Meg had a brother, Jake, who lived in a place called Atlanta in the state of Georgia. Jake and his wife had two children. 'I love kids!' Meg declared often, sometimes in the middle of nothing. She was, herself, in relationship—a *committed* relationship—with a man named Luke. 'He's a typical guy,' she would say. 'Terrified of marriage. Anyways.' She was hoping to get married after finishing her nursing degree. 'I want lots of kids! I just can't help it. I see kids and I think—gotta get me some of those!'

Prema found Americans so curious she could not help studying each one.

Her other housemate, Susan Kitterow, was in her forties, with crimped blond hair and a trim figure. Discounting the ageing around her eyes, Susan was attractive in the way of fashion models. She was originally from the state of Idaho, and had lived in the city of Seattle, in the state of Washington, before moving south for the sun, she said. Susan was sugary—she called Prema 'honey'—but they rarely met, as she worked long hours at a health food store. When she was home she brewed organic beer, batch upon batch left to ferment in holding tanks in the kitchen. Most evenings she went on dates, staying out all night or bringing back a man who would invariably leave early the next morning. Sometimes Prema only heard these men's voices through the walls. With Meg and Prema, Susan referred to these men only by nicknames. 'I'm going out with the tax man,' she would say, or, 'The biker's got a bubble-butt.'

When Susan was not around Meg made disparaging comments about what she called Susan's 'lifestyle choices', but to Prema it was intriguing. 'Mr Rosé's such a hottie,' Susan would sigh, or, 'I could lick ice cream off the Beemer hunk all day.' Though Susan never said anything bad about the men, she seemed to form no attachments to them; she only had sex with them. Casual sex. Though there was, once, one man whom she dated for two weeks. The panther, she called him, although when Prema saw him he looked more like a brown bear. Susan looked happy enough while he was around, but after he stopped coming she told Meg, who told Prema, that his neediness had been toxic.

Meg and Susan both had cars; they came and went as they pleased, day or night. In the evenings Prema was alone at home. After dinner she would watch television: car races, court cases, news of celebrity couplings and separations, ads for colonic irrigations, weight-loss breakthroughs and reverse mortgages with tax-free proceeds. Inanities. Or she would read in her room, or look past the window's iron grills through her binoculars. A young, good-looking Latino couple lived in the house across, with three high-spirited, giggly daughters. They seemed like an ideal family. An old black lady lived by herself in an adjacent brick house. Prema had never seen her leave her house. In a few of the other houses Prema could see the flicker of a television screen at a window, or the occasional movement of a person. Her neighbours.

A Whole Other Life

~

It was a zigzag trail that had landed her on the dry, grassy hill, the same trail that had led her out of her birth village to the capital, then to the hill bazaar.

Some weeks after Prema joined the green-card lottery, Rajan came by the bazaar, and they walked together to the town at the base of the hills, along a stone trail lined by crown-of-thorn shrubs. Springtime had arrived, and the terraced fields were greening. Some bazaar-dwellers overtook them going down, others passed them going up. It was customary to greet even strangers: 'Heading down?' 'Walk carefully.' 'Go well.'

The town at the base of the hills was not big, but it was labyrinthine enough for them to lose themselves in. They made their way to the Maya Lodge, tucked into a back alleyway. The lodge's proprietor was shelling peas on the front porch. He smiled when he saw them: 'Oho, Sir, Sister. Welcome back. The neighbours cut a goat this morning: there'll be stew for dinner tonight. Go on up,' he said. 'The rooms are all vacant, take any two.'

For the sake of decorum, Rajan and Prema always claimed to be in town for work. If the proprietor had wanted to find out the truth, he could have, of course; but either he did not want to, or he already knew and didn't care to let on. Their lie was convenient for them all.

Prema took her usual room on the top floor, a room with a view of corrugated tin roofs. Rajan took the room directly below, and came up in a while.

Though he headed the poverty-alleviation programme, Rajan disagreed with the policies that the head office, in the capital, set. 'An accountant from the head office calls and says: Give women interest-free loans,' he said, flopping down on the bed beside Prema. His wide-set eyes darted impatiently. 'Why? Because a Danish aid agency gave us some money and said: Give poor women interest-free loans. So you find some poor women and force them to take loans, even though they'd rather you built them an irrigation canal.' He laughed, but drily, without humour. 'And you?' he asked. 'You've erased your British company's carbon footprints?'

'The forest users' committee fined a low-caste widow who stole into the forest to gather some kindling,' Prema said.

'Development!' he said. 'A farce!'

By and by they talked about everything that had happened since their last assignation, starting with the grosser events and moving on to the finer emotions. Prema told Rajan about the preparations for the wedding of the schoolteacher couple's daughter, about the way she had lost her balance when returning from the plantation: 'There was an earthquake. That may have been why I slipped. Did you feel it?'

'No.'

'Neither did I. Apparently it was quite big.'

Rajan ran his hands through Prema's hair, listening to her talk; then he told her about his days.

They were never in a hurry to make love, but when they did, it was with tenderness. At some point, he took her in his arms and kissed her. They moved their hands over each other, taking off their clothes, reacquainting themselves with their nakedness. Rajan was the only man Prema had made love with. She did not think she was his first lover, though she did not know for sure. When they were ready he would reach into a pocket of his tossed-aside shirt for a condom. The walls of the lodge were made of plywood, so the only sounds they made as they joined were their breathing, their gasping.

Afterwards, they lay in bed talking. Rajan was passionate about politics. As a student he had joined a communist student union, organizing demonstrations and strikes, fighting face-to-face with policemen, courting tear gas, beatings, arrest. He had spent two months in jail during the last movement for democracy. Afterwards, his party had been rocked by corruption scandals, and he had quit, disillusioned. Now here he was, working for a non-government organization—shackled, Prema felt, to a job he didn't believe in. When they had first met—at a staff seminar hosted by the head office in the capital—she had seen him glance past their colleagues. He had sat near the door as though wanting to leave. When officials from the head office had talked about poverty alleviation his gaze had slid afar. Prema had thought him cynical at first; but as she got to know him she realized that he wanted to do more than implement a few spotty projects here and there. He still dreamed of structural change, of revolution.

That evening he talked about the possibility of a ceasefire. The Maoist rebels were in favour of it, he said; their troops were wearying and they wanted to initiate peace talks. But the king, backed by the army, was refusing: 'They've got India, America giving them M-16s. Ten thousand people have died, but they want more bloodshed. The king and the army are using the war to keep themselves in power.'

His conviction was a clear, flowing stream.

At eight, they went down to the dining hall and had dinner. By eight-thirty they were back in Prema's room. She told him about the green-card lottery at that point. Rajan asked how it worked, and she explained: 'They draw numbers, and one or two thousand people get to go to America.'

'I didn't know you wanted to go abroad,' he said.

'I don't,' she said.

'Everyone wants to go abroad,' he said.

'I don't,' she said.

Changing the topic, she told him about the photograph of the Mongolian family in the newspaper: 'They were eating momos. My mouth watered just looking at them.'

'I've been there,' he said.

'Where?'

'Mongolia. Years ago. The Party sent us.'

Rajan was like that, facts about him dropped casually into his conversations—like his being colour-blind, which he had mentioned as an aside only a few weeks ago.

Prema sat up in bed. 'What was it like?'

Rajan was lying on his back, gazing at the ceiling with a faraway expression. 'There were two of us, both student activists. We went together,' he said. 'First we took the bus to Delhi, to meet up with other students from India. Then we all flew to Poland.'

'You've been to Poland too?'

'Just for a few days. From there we flew to Moscow and stayed overnight. We flew to Ulan Bator the next day.'

'What was it like?'

'Cold! Parched. Horrible weather. We spent all our time in a concrete-block building with local student activists, hardly left it at all, except on the last day. They took us to see a traditional Mongolian house. It turned out to be a tent!'

'Is Mongolia like those parts of Tibet,' Prema asked, 'where one girl marries several men?'

But Rajan was lost in his own thoughts: 'They're called ger, those tents. Like ghar: Home. There's everything in them: a kitchen, a table, beds, even a television. You wouldn't think it would be comfortable, but there's everything there. Some of the local activists were saying we could live in a tent like that if we wanted to stay on.' He said, 'Can you imagine what my life would have been like, love, if I had stayed? I would have had a whole other life.'

A whole other life. Prema had never been to another country, not even to India, nearby, or to Tibet. China. She knew Rajan considered the United States an aggressor in the world: a country unaccountable for its excesses and atrocities, an agent of— corporate capitalist expansionism. Something like that.

'Would it be wrong to go to America?' she asked. 'If I were to win the lottery, I mean?'

He shrugged. 'In these days of transnationalism.'

She could not tell what he meant.

He said, 'Did you bring your radio? Turn it on, love. It's time for the national news.'

They listened to reports on the latest skirmishes between the army and the Maoist rebels.

In the Old-Growth Forest

~

Prema had always admired Rajan's ardency, his conviction. She did not share all his beliefs, but that did not matter. Between them, they joked that his interests lay with human beings, and hers with everything else. The natural world.

Yet this was not quite true. Forestry, as Prema had learned it in college, amounted to the administration of timber. She had chosen the field out of pragmatic concerns rather than out of any special calling. She had not felt it possible to even do such a thing; for it had seemed to her that people like her—who had known early of the world's sorrows—did not *choose* what to become. They survived; and if lucky, they progressed. She had survived; she had progressed. She had found work as a conservationist. Did she *believe* in conservation? Generally, yes, of course. Her generation had come into a world bemoaning its own destruction. But specifically? Because of her education, she knew more about flora, the sustainers of life—the providers—than about fauna, the consumers. She did not know enough about the natural sciences—botany, biology, biogeography—or about the interconnections, dependencies and linkages of the natural world, to have much of a feel for it.

And it was not easy to gain such a feel. When she had taken

this job, she had thought she would be spending time in the wilderness; but her work kept her mostly in the bazaar. High above the bazaar was an old-growth forest where ancient birches were said to grow dense and gnarled. Though it was part of the conservation programme to monitor the old-growth forest, neither Trailokya nor Prema had ever ventured there, as that was where the Maoist rebels were said to be camped. Unlike in Prema's birth village, the Maoist rebels rarely came into the hill bazaar. The few who did were unarmed. Prema instinctively recoiled at the thought of encountering them, though she could not also help wondering what they were like, these rebels to whom her sister had surrendered her fate.

Now and again, a rebel commander came into the bazaar, a twenty-year-old who went by the alias Samaanata: equality. He had a doctrinaire air. One day he visited Trailokya and Prema in the room they rented as an office. Over tea he asked, politely enough, about the organization's work, inquiring about the size of the budget and explaining, quietly but insistently, that non-government organizations were not revolutionary; they were moderate, reformist. 'At the start our struggle was limited to a few areas,' he told them gravely, 'but now it is nationwide. You must support us. When we are victorious there will be a great task before educated people like yourselves. You must help us build a new society along revolutionary lines.'

'Yes, of course,' Trailokya said, just to appease him.

Prema wondered whether her sister, too, entertained such grandiose visions. Out of curiosity, she asked the rebel commander about his—and his comrades'—views on conservation.

He had to think about it. 'The people,' he said tentatively, 'should control their natural resources.' Then, more confidently, he said, 'The centre has always exploited the peripheries. It is a matter of historical redress. All this'—he gestured at the hills outside the window—'belongs to the people. The people at the peripheries should benefit from their use.' He glanced over for confirmation. 'Isn't that so, Sister?'

It was a common enough functionalist view. 'You see nature as a resource for people,' Prema said. 'It is the same belief as that of our organization.'

The rebel commander shook his head. 'But your organization is reformist. Whereas our path is revolutionary.'

Prema demurred. Wasn't everyone—revolutionary or reformist, or even reactionary—in the death grip of nature? It seemed shortsighted to claim ownership over what you could not control. She did not say this, of course. She did not dare to.

But after this meeting with Samaanata, she felt emboldened. Perhaps there was no need to fear the Maoists. Perhaps they were all—like him—doctrinaire, but polite enough.

As spring progressed, the hill bazaar was covered with a riot of peach and plum blossoms that crowded the trees till their petals dropped, one by one, covering the ground. Rain clouds drifted through the sky and gathered at the edge of the himals. The monsoon would not be long now. It would be impossible to go into the old-growth forests once the rains came.

And so early one Saturday morning Prema packed some bread and a thermos of tea in a rucksack and set out at sunrise, binoculars in hand. Past the slumbering bazaar she crossed the gully and soon reached the plantation. Beyond that lay what Trailokya and she had set up as a 'buffer zone', a patch of forest from where the bazaar-dwellers were allowed to gather a fixed quota of firewood and fodder. The forests beyond were wild, and off-limits for use.

Prema took a narrow footpath along a rocky incline, past wide, leafy oaks and narrow alders. As she walked uphill, dragonflies buzzed past and gnats danced in the sunlight. The vegetation altered as the air thinned. Broadleaf trees gave way to junipers and larches and silver firs. The ground grew hard and rocky. The morning wore on. The sun bore down with a tropical intensity. It took her four hours to reach the first of the birches.

There, in the sparkling high-altitude air, she lay low on the ground to rest awhile. There was a fluttering in a nearby branch, and a snap of twigs, a scuttling in the underbrush. Serenity. A woodpecker was perched on a hemlock, worrying at its trunk. High above, an eagle was looping through the sky. A bald eagle? A great eagle. Through the binoculars Prema followed its loops through the viewfinder—and caught a flare on the edge of the viewfinder: orange, like the blaze of a matchstick. An explosion? It fizzled away into nothingness. She waited for an accompanying bang, but heard none. Had it been a missile or a grenade? A bomb or a gun? Fireworks? A meteor?

She was still scanning the sky when she heard footsteps. A man had turned a corner and appeared on the footpath. Behind him came another man, and then another. Others followed: fifteen or twenty, marching single-file directly towards her. The man in front had a rifle slung across his back.

Prema stood up, her heart pounding. The man at the head of the group saw her, and pulled on a stony expression. He marched by without further acknowledgement. The others, too, marched by in complete silence. Some were just boys—and girls. Two girls had short-cropped hair. Maoist rebels. They were carrying rifles. None of them so much as glanced at Prema, as though she were an apparition—or they were.

Soon they dipped past a bend in the trail.

Her sister Bijaya.

Prema lost the nerve to stay on.

Rushing back down the hill, she cursed her sister. The idiot girl. Where was she now? Did she really believe in war? The idiot, idiot girl.

A girl no longer a girl: Bijaya would be seventeen now, the age Prema had been when she had left home. That was the last time she had seen Bijaya. A neighbour was going to the capital; Prema was going with him, to live in a girls' hostel near her college campus. Prema's father prepared the morning meal that day. 'I've had to be both father and mother to you, Chhori,' he said, serving her, squatting on his haunches at the hearth, watching her eat. He had aged rapidly as a widower, his face sunken and his muscles loose over a bony frame. 'Your mother should have lived to see this day,' he said. 'To see you going to college! By her blessings, you will progress, Chhori. You will lead a complete life.'

Afterwards, he placed a teeka of red powder on her forehead, and a garland of marigolds around her neck. The neighbour was waiting. Bijaya had gone to fetch water that morning and hadn't come back. Or she was keeping away. She had been quieter than usual over the past few days, upset, maybe, over her sister's departure. It was difficult to know.

Prema didn't want to leave without saying goodbye to her. She checked behind the house and circled the small plot of land on which it stood, but Bijaya was not there. She went back into the house and looked through the rooms. At the shrine in her parents' room, she picked up her mother's ammonite and slipped it into her pocket. Then she went outside again.

'We should leave,' the neighbour said. 'The walk alone will take six, seven hours, and it's best to find lodgings before dark, so we can get up early for tomorrow's bus ride.'

'Just a bit longer,' Prema pleaded.

Again, she circled the house, and this time, she saw Bijaya in the bamboo grove beyond the Shiva-Parvati temple. The girl was doing nothing. Just staring at the terraced rice fields beyond.

Prema went to the grove. The wind was rippling through the bamboo, a susurration. Bijaya glanced up as Prema approached.

'I'm leaving, Bahini. I wanted to—'

Bijaya's eyes were glittery with rage. She hissed, 'You're never coming back, are you?'

It took Prema a while to respond: 'Of course I will. I'll come back every chance I get.'

'You're leaving me,' Bijaya cried. She let out a gasp, as though choking. Then she said: 'What's it like in the cities? It can't be like this'—she gestured furiously at the fields. 'What's it like?'

'I don't know,' Prema said.

'I hate where we're from,' Bijaya hissed.

She was right: Prema had never gone back. Rushing downhill now, Prema left the junipers and larches and silver firs behind, re-entering the lower ranges with oaks and alders. At the very edge of the buffer zone, she saw an animal loping across the footpath. A wildcat: small and pale, spotted, with sharp ears, large paws and a black-tipped tail.

It stopped when it heard her.

She stopped too, out of fear.

For an instant, their eyes met. And Prema felt something in that instant, something calming, something corrective.

Then the cat turned away and darted out of sight.

Back at the office, Prema consulted a field guide and found out it had been a lynx.

No Soy Mexicana

~

Since then, Prema had not been back in a wilderness, either in Nepal or in America. The closest she had got was the Los Angeles coastline. All of Esther's neighbourhood had a frayed, weather-beaten quality, the houses all nestling into the bluff, as though sheltering. The street lamps were chipped, the street signs were flaking. Weeds colonized every crack in the road, and the breeze carried the ocean's scent like a memory.

The winter passed—Prema's third winter in this land—neither cold nor warm, with occasional showers that tinged the land green. Whenever the weather was clear she would take Esther to the beach for lunch. Her own skin darkened with exposure. She came to recognize pelicans, cormorants, sanderlings. Shorebirds and waterbirds. She began to note the coincidence of the tide and the moonrise, and to wonder at the life in the splash zone and the depths, of the tidal zones churning murkily with giant kelp, anemones, nudibranches. As the weather warmed, people began to go into the water. One day she saw an entire family running towards the rising waves, then running back, squealing, as the waves chased them. Wasn't the water polluted? Didn't the chemical run-off of the metropolis end up here? Nobody seemed bothered by the drainpipe at the centre of the sand, spewing brown liquids. A pier had been laid on top of the drainpipe. One day Prema saw a man and a woman standing on it, kissing.

Every other week a van would come to take Esther for a check-up. The driver would strap in her wheelchair, help Prema in, and tear at top speed through the freeway to Meadowvale, a nursing home on a southern peninsula. There the driver would help Esther out, and Prema would take her in.

Prema had never, until entering Meadowvale, been inside the type of building that fended off the weather. To her, this metropolis seemed defenceless against the sun and the wind. The dust. At Meadowvale the door glided open to the hum of central air conditioning. An orderly at the registration desk checked Esther in, then wheeled her off to the doctor. Prema waited in a lobby bright with fluorescent lights, multicoloured vinyl sofas and coffee tables stacked with glossy brochures. Classical music wafted from concealed speakers.

She learned from the glossy brochure that Esther was enrolled in the Assisted Home Living Program here, which covered the cost of her check-ups. If her health deteriorated, she could be upgraded to the Live-in Independence Program and moved to a flat on the premises. 'It's a pricey asylum, dear,' Esther had sniffed while waiting for the van the first time. To Prema, though… An exclusive private concern, Meadowvale was part of a nationwide chain boasting top-notch geriatric services. So claimed its glossy brochure. And though paying for care was probably not as desirable as having your family care for you, if you did not have family and if you could afford it, this seemed a tidy way of preparing for old age, sickness, death. Prema could not help wishing for it for her father.

It was at Meadowvale that Prema met Luis. He was the general administrator of the nursing home, with a desk set away from the registration desk. It was not part of his job to handle outpatients, but he was the kind of administrator who made an extra effort. On one of her early visits he came by to greet Esther: 'Morning there, Mrs King, and how are you doing today?'

'Young Mr Reyes!' Esther beamed. 'My, aren't you looking dashing today!'

'You should tell that to my ex-wife!' Luis nodded at Prema: 'Hola, me llamo Luis.' Then he turned back to Esther: 'You ready to meet Doctor Ismaili, Mrs King? He's ready and waiting for you.'

As Luis reached over to help the orderly with Esther's wheelchair, Prema saw a bracelet on his wrist, a bracelet with a locket bearing the face of a Hindu guru. The guru who had been charged with conspiracy to murder back when she lived in the hill bazaar.

After the orderly had wheeled Esther away, Luis turned to her. '¿Quieres tomar un café?'

'No soy Mexicana,' she said, having learned early on how to deal with this confusion.

'¡Ni yo!' He laughed. '¡Soy cien por ciento Americano!'

She had to explain: 'No habla Español.'

'¿De verdad?' He looked her up and down. 'Geez, sorry about that, I could have sworn— I was just saying, kinigitchyacoffee?'

'Pardon?'

'Or a soda? The vending machine's got 7 Ups.'

'Oh.' Prema finally caught on. 'No, thank you.'

Luis was not cinema-hero handsome, but he had a likeable face, an easy smile and liquid, honey-brown eyes. 'Hey, I didn't catch your name,' he said.

'Prema.'

He raised an eyebrow. 'As in "love" in Saanz-kreet?'

She nodded warily, recalling the locket of the guru.

'You're not going to tell me you're from India, are you? Can I tell you something?' he said, stepping in confidingly. 'Don't laugh, okay? Promise you won't laugh?'

'All right.'

He said, 'I have an India calling.'

She did not understand the expression.

He got a dreamy look in his eyes. 'It's like—I have to go over there some day, to Reesh-kesh or Haar-dwaar, with all those hermits meditating in caves. Like something's saying, yo Luis, get yourself over here, pronto. Is that crazy?'

Prema baulked. 'I am from Nepal actually.'

'Whoa.' He stepped back and stared at her in wide-eyed wonder. 'I never met anyone from Nepal. Hey, you're my first Nepalese.'

Prema was not enjoying this conversation. 'Nepali,' she said.

'What?'

'Not Nepalese. Nepali.'

'Sorry. Nepali,' he said. 'You're my first.'

With an abruptness she had not quite intended, she replied, 'Sorry to say you are not my first American.'

He laughed. 'That's good,' he said. 'We Americans, we're a dime a dozen around here. So Prema, you working for Mrs King, huh? See you around?'

'Bye.'

Two weeks later, Esther had lunch with a family friend who was a resident at Meadowvale. 'Donald's deaf as a stone and not all there,' Esther said while getting dressed. This did not keep her from selecting an especially flowery dress that morning, and daubing pink lipstick just as the van arrived.

Over lunch at the Meadowvale cafeteria, Esther babbled: 'The universe is offering you pentacles, the fortune teller said! Timmy didn't believe, of course. Said it was all mumbo jumbo. But then we went to Cairo.' Donald sat across from her, impassive. Impossible to know if he was following her. Not that Esther noticed: 'It's all in your mind, Timmy said. You know how Timmy was. A Virgo, with Leo rising…'

She was forgetting to eat. Prema nudged her. 'Esther, please have some soup.'

'The best fortune teller in London!'

Just then Luis tapped Prema on the shoulder. 'Hey, Prema. Remember me? Me llamo Luis? Siwidja?'

'Pardon?'

'If that seat's not taken, that is.'

'No. Yes. You can sit on it,' Prema said.

As before, Luis made a poor impression. Right off, he told her he had a real thing for mountains. 'I'd love to go to the Himmel-*aa*-yas. They must be amazing. I mean, I saw a programme on TV, and there they were, so majestic. Right there in front of you.' He sighed. 'The Himmel-*aa*-yas.'

'Himals,' Prema said.

'Sorry?'

'Him*aa*ls. Him*aa*layas.' She turned to Esther. 'Esther, have some soup.'

Esther finally took a spoonful to her mouth, but put it down without so much as tasting it: 'Donald, do you remember the ambassador's daughter?'

'Is that how you say it?' Luis said. 'The himmels?'

'They are pretty to look at,' Prema replied, 'but not so easy to live near.'

'Right.' He said, 'I was reading there was some trouble in Nepal. Some killings or something? Some fighting?'

'A war.'

'A *war* war, like a real war, huh. Is it safe?'

'Tourists can trek to the Mount Everest base camp.'

'Mount Everest, wow! You ever been?'

'No.'

'Man, I'd love to go!'

Luis had a disarming way of blurting out what was personal, what was private. After confessing that his interest in mountains was actually spiritual, he began to talk about what he called his practice: 'Twenty minutes every morning, you sit with your eyes closed and meditate. It's real good for you. But you must know all that.'

'I am not religious,' Prema said.

'It's not like I am either. Though you know? I went to a Hindu temple once. In Hollywood, believe it? At first it was weird, but then—' He got a dreamy look. 'All those voices in harmony. I felt something. There was a real power in those chants.'

To this Prema had no response.

'Well. Gotta get back to work.' He stood up. 'See you next time, Prema?'

'Bye.'

A Letter from an Americané

~

Rare though it was to meet an American who knew anything about Nepal, it did not occur to Prema that she and Luis would be friends. His notion of Nepal was…touristy. Americans did not know where she was from. There was not enough commonality to base a friendship on. In anything other than friendship, Prema was not interested: in dating, or in having an American relationship. She had already had American sex once, and had found it wanting in love. As for love: it was enough to have had an attachment to one person, and to have left him.

Rajan.

The monsoon arrived not long after Prema's trip to the old-growth forest. The rains drenched the hill bazaar, slowing down the pace of work. This was a slack time in the organization, a time for writing progress reports about the year that had passed, and drafting plans and proposals for the upcoming year. One lazy afternoon, as the rain drummed against the windowpane in a dense white spray, Kanchha burst into the office, draped head to toe in a plastic sheet. Trailokya had taken the day off. Prema was alone, reading a glossy World Wildlife Fund brochure that the head office had sent. From below the plastic sheet Kanchha produced an envelope. 'A letter, Sister! A letter for you, from an Americané!'

He watched Prema read the letter.

It was from a servicing centre in the state of Kentucky, in America. Her name had been selected in the preliminary round. She would be informed if she made the final selection. After that she would be able to apply for legal permanent residency.

Prema quickly put the letter away.

'What is it, Sister?' Kanchha asked.

'It's about office work,' she lied.

He gave her a knowing look. 'From an Americané?'

'It's about office work,' she said.

'Tell me honestly,' he said.

'I'm telling you honestly,' she insisted.

The boy pouted. Prema knew he didn't believe her; but she also knew that if she told him the truth he would tell the entire bazaar, and she didn't want that, not when she hardly knew, herself, what this meant.

She watched Kanchha run back out into the pelting rain.

For several days she read and reread the letter, wondering what to make of it. Then, one day, she went to the cybercafe, to try to find out more. Kanchha was helping a teenage girl and her parents Skype-phone a relative abroad. When he became free, Prema told the boy that she needed to place a call.

'A call to the Americané embassy?' he asked.

'A call about work,' she said. 'It's about office work.'

Prema entered the glass confines of the telephone booth as the boy stood by, staring at her in undisguised curiosity.

She called the American embassy in the capital, and past the automated instructions eventually reached a man. But the line was bad; she could barely hear him speaking. 'Hello! Hello?' He said something—'The American'—then there was a sputter of static. 'Can you hear me? Hello?'

She replied, 'Yes, hello.'

In her halting, unpractised college English, she told him about the letter she had received. 'Can you tell me what it means?'

The man turned out to be a compatriot. He switched effortlessly to Nepali: 'You're telling me your name has been drawn in the diversity visa lottery? You must understand—' The line popped and whizzed, and Prema thought he had hung up. But then she heard: 'Then we do the pre-screening. Hello? Can you hear me?'

He told her that if she made the final selection, she would get an appointment at the embassy. She would have her application pre-screened there. Only if she met the criteria would she be advised to apply for permanent residency. He rattled off a list of documents that she would have to bring. 'Proof of financial self-sufficiency. Police certificate. Medical test,' he said, over the crackling static. 'Do you understand?'

'Yes,' she said, though she did not quite.

'Let me assure you that the embassy will extend'—static—'a success. But please understand—' Something. Then: 'Good luck.'

'Thank you.'

Kanchha sidled up to her as she left the glass booth. 'What did they say, Sister? What did they say? Did they say you're going to get a green card?'

'They said I need to get back to work.'

Some weeks later she got a second letter from the servicing station in the state of Kentucky.

'I suppose this is also about work?' Kanchha said pointedly, handing it to her.

The letter confirmed her selection.

Prema told Rajan about all this the next time they were together at the Maya Lodge. She showed both letters to him, and told him that she would have to go to the embassy, in the capital, for a pre-screening appointment. 'Will you go with me?' she asked.

'To Kathmandu?' he said. 'All right.'

She realized that she hadn't asked him to go to America. If they married, he might be eligible to apply…They were sitting on the bed in the room with a view on to corrugated tin roofs. 'Don't tell anyone.' she said.

'That you're going to the capital?' he said.

'No, to America.'

'You're definitely going?'

'I haven't even applied yet. The application— They can turn you down even after you apply.' She attempted humour: 'Kanchha's banner was wrong, it's not automatically guaranteed.'

But Rajan wanted to know: 'If your application is accepted, you'll go?'

'I don't know.'

More tenderly, he asked, 'You've consulted your father?'

'No.'

'Have you heard from your sister at all?'

'No.'

He looked at her, his wide-set eyes searching her face. Then he said, 'I won't tell anyone.' And this became another secret, like their assignations, that they kept from everyone around them.

Even years later, Prema could not be sure whether what she and Rajan had had was what Americans would call a relationship.

There was an attachment, she knew. She would have liked to keep that. She assumed he would have wanted so, too. Yet— Can we ever know the depths of an other? In the two years that Rajan and she had been intimate, the issue of the future had never arisen between them. Perhaps he was uncertain, or she was. Although well into the age of an arranged marriage, Prema had no desire to find a husband. A dread seeped through her at the thought of childbirth. She had seen it consume her mother. In the years following her death, Prema had spent hours in the bamboo grove, cursing her mother's frailty, vowing to be flinty, strong. And she had become so. She had rejected her mother's faith in the gods. She had gone to college, whereas her mother had not passed out of high school. She worked, she was modern. In no way had she replicated her mother's life. Not that— The subject of marriage had never come up between her and Rajan. Prema had not raised it. And Rajan had never brought it up either. If Rajan felt any conflict about her going to America, it did not show now. But then many things did not show on him; this did not mean he didn't feel them. She was like that too. A survivor above all. She did not want to lose Rajan; but she did not let this show.

In time she received notice of her pre-screening appointment at the American embassy. A few days earlier, she and Rajan took leave from work, and, from the town at the base of the hills, caught an overnight bus to the capital. There they checked into an anonymous lodge in the tourist district, the Kathmandu Hotel.

It took some effort to gather the documents she needed: queuing up at the police station, getting checked by a physician.

She added their reports to the documents of her life—attestations, certificates, degrees. Then she went to the embassy for her appointment.

Past a security check for which she had to take off her shoes, she was met by a smartly suited man—a compatriot, though he behaved like a foreigner. He led her through a clipped garden into a fortress-like building. It was spotless inside, as Prema imagined America itself would be. The office room smelled lemony and disinfected. At his desk the man flipped through her documents with practice.

'Birth certificate. High school...and college degree. Good. Police clearance. Only for Nepal? You've never lived elsewhere? Doctor's report. Good. What's the date on that? Good. Bank statement? Sponsor letter?' He said, 'You have to furnish proof of financial self-sufficiency, or your application will be rejected. A bank statement or a sponsor letter from someone in America will do. What's this? Ah, your bank statement.'

He then checked her application form, circling all the mistakes. 'Here you have to list every address you've lived at since the age of eighteen. And here you have to list all the jobs you've ever held. There should be no gaps in the time frame. None. And where in America do you intend to live? You'll have to put that down here. Here. Just the name of the place will do.'

Unable to think of any place, Prema put down the capital, Washington D.C.

The man made her redo the entire application. At the end he made her sign it. 'We'll pass the file on,' he said, tucking everything into an envelope. 'This was just the pre-screening, mind. Next comes the actual interview. We'll let you know the date. You'll have to pay the application fee then. Seven seventy-five dollars. Can be its equivalent in rupees, but cash only, please. That's seven hundred and seventy-five dollars.'

She was at the embassy for nearly two hours. In that time Rajan had borrowed a motorcycle from a friend. He was waiting for her when she came out of the embassy gates.

'Finished?'

'Finished.'

From there they went on a ride through the city, she sitting pillion behind him, holding tightly as he sped by billboards advertising whisky, watches, condoms. They drove past the royal palace to a broad avenue where a peace movement was being staged in those days. Daily, labour union members, students, political activists, human rights defenders, teachers and lawyers gathered here to press the king and the army for peace talks with the Maoist rebels. The king and the army accused these activists of abetting the rebels. Sometimes there were crackdowns. The police would fire tear gas to disperse the crowds, and the demonstrators would respond by hurling rocks or burning tyres. The avenue would descend into anarchy.

That day there was a thin gathering of boys about a lone banner: CIVIL SOCIETY MOVEMENT. Riot police were watching, unnerved, as some boys set fire to an effigy of the king. Rajan found out from one of the boys that the day's demonstrations had ended. There had been a few scuffles, nothing serious. 'Looks like we missed it,' he said wistfully.

After they got back to the Kathmandu Hotel, he asked Prema, again, how things had gone at the embassy.

'Fine,' she said.

'There was no difficulty?'

'No.'

They did not talk further about it. She was, in truth, struggling to discover how she felt. She was getting a chance to leave one life and start another one. Did she want another life?

Did Rajan?

The next morning they returned the motorbike, and then walked back through the town to the tourist district, stopping, for a treat, at the international ice cream chain, Baskin-Robbins. Then they checked out of the Kathmandu Hotel and took the bus back to the town at the base of the hills.

'Are you all right?' Rajan kept asking during the ride.

'I'm fine. You?'

'I'm all right.'

Something inside Prema had changed, though. Something inside her had hardened. Back in the hill bazaar, she went through her days as usual, but alone in her room each night, she held on to her mother's ammonite, feeling its shale-coloured exterior, and opening it with a clack to examine the fossilized exoskeleton inside.

A whole other life.

When the monsoon rains ceased the organization's work resumed at full pace. The schoolteacher couple's youngest daughter got married to much fanfare on a sun-soaked day at the end of summer. The terraced fields surrounding the bazaar gradually ripened. Trailokya's infant son learned to crawl. Rajan and Prema continued to go to the Maya Lodge every few weeks. They would make love as before and lie in bed talking as though nothing had changed between them. Yet the thought—'I am leaving'—was akin to awareness of an impending death. It altered everything. Till she had won the green-card lottery Prema had been content enough, having wrested a middle-class life out of a childhood of poverty. There was nothing wrong with what she had. Yet it seemed she wanted more.

The Boy Who Disappeared

~

Or she lacked the heart to stay. At the start of autumn, an army patrol came to the hill bazaar. It was a lazy Saturday morning. Prema was sitting on the porch with the schoolteacher couple, talking about their daughter, who was already pregnant. 'If it's a son, her in-laws won't pressure her to have more children,' the wife was explaining. 'It's not that I wouldn't want a granddaughter—girl, boy, what difference to progressives like us? It's just that her in-laws…'

Just then the husband drew a sharp breath.

Two columns of men were filing into the bazaar, sixty or seventy in total. They were in civilian dress, and yet they were armed with rifles. Their bearing—their buzz cuts—had a cold military air. They stopped at a clearing at the bazaar centre. A hush fell as the bazaar-dwellers gathered uneasily at their doors.

At the centre the patrol split into teams of four, fanning out through the bazaar. Prema and the schoolteacher couple got up in alarm as the team came to their house.

The soldier heading the team cast a dull eye over them, lingering over Prema. He spat, pushed a wad of tobacco into his cheek, and drawled, 'Are there Maoists in the bazaar?'

The husband replied for them: 'We don't have dealings with such people, Sah'b. We never have. Never.'

'They must come by sometimes,' he said, still looking Prema over.

'We don't know anything, Sah'b.'

He glanced at the schoolteacher couple, then turned back to Prema. 'Who's she?' he asked.

The wife answered: 'She's our younger sister, our Bahini, Sah'b. She works here, she teaches us to look after our jungles. She's not a Maoist, Sah'b.'

'Got any identification?' the soldier asked Prema.

From her room Prema fetched her citizenship certificate and staff ID card.

The soldier looked them over, resumed chewing, and turned away.

The rest of the team went into the house and searched through the rooms, turning everything upside down, looking, presumably, for some evidence of Maoist presence. They found none. Then they moved on to the next house.

They repeated this routine at every house, till, an hour later, a team dragged a boy out of the cybercafe, shouting abuses: 'Saala chuthiya chor!'

It was Kanchha they were dragging.

The atmosphere in the bazaar grew tense. The bazaar-dwellers watched as the boy writhed in the soldiers' grasp, screaming: 'Let me go, let me go, let me go!' His father, the retired Gurkha soldier, ran behind, pleading: 'There's been a mistake, Sah'b, he's not a Maoist, he's my son, let him be!' The soldiers paid no attention to him. At the centre of the bazaar they hurled Kanchha on to the ground. 'Where are they, saala? Chuthiya! Tell us where they are!'

Then they set upon him.

Beside Prema, the schoolteacher wife screamed: 'Lau na! Lau na!'

'He's my son, Sah'b, he's not a Maoist! Spare him!'

From Kanchha came a high animal yelp.

'Sah'b, he's only fourteen, let him be!'

'Shut up or we'll finish you too, old man!'

A team of soldiers stormed the cybercafe, smashing the glass partitions and wrecking the interior. Eventually everyone from the patrol regrouped where Kanchha lay, crumpled and groaning. 'Get up, saala! Up, up!' They dragged him off the ground, then left, prodding him along.

After they were gone, some of the bazaar-dwellers crept back into their homes in fear. Others rushed out to where Kanchha's father stood, looking lost. The schoolteacher couple ran to his side. Prema followed. The cybercafe's front door was broken, the ATOMATIC GARANTEE GREEN CARD banner ripped and dangling. The matron who ran the teashop stood by, shouting: 'If they wanted the boy why not just take the boy? Why beat him? Why smash the computers? Savages!' A crowd thickened around Kanchha's father. For a while Prema stood there. Then—not seeing what she could do to help—she retreated.

That night she listened to the radio with the schoolteacher couple. 'Kanchha' merely meant 'youngest son'; the boy's proper name was Suk Bahadur Ale. There was no mention of a Suk Bahadur Ale on the local or the national news. This was not unusual. There had been thousands of such army arrests—abductions—during the course of the war, and few had ever made the news.

The following morning, Kanchha's father went to the town at the base of the hills hoping to discover his son's whereabouts. He returned at dusk with no real answers. He had gone, first, to the jailhouse in town. The policeman on duty had told him to go to the army barracks. But the soldiers at the barracks had said there was no Suk Bahadur Ale in their custody. So he had returned to the jailhouse and talked to the policeman again, even meeting a high-ranking inspector this time. They had insisted that the boy was in army custody. Some of the townspeople who lived near the barracks had also told him that they had seen a captive brought here the previous day. But back at the barracks, the soldiers had once again sworn they were not holding the boy.

'What kind of army, police—?' Kanchha's father wailed before a gaping crowd. 'Could he help it if the Maoists came to the cybercafe? Is that his fault? Does that make him a Maoist too? They just took him,' he wailed.

Kanchha's abduction disheartened Prema, and made her withdraw into herself. It had the opposite effect on Rajan. The outrage energized him. The following day, having heard what had happened, he came to the hill bazaar. 'You can't just arrest someone, even if he is a Maoist,' he told Kanchha's father. 'You need an arrest warrant. You have to follow due process.' He convinced the former Gurkha soldier to file a case. Rajan even went, himself, to the town at the base of the hills, to consult a lawyer friend there. He returned at nightfall with the lawyer's promise to file a habeas corpus writ pro bono. 'We'll get your son out, Ba,' he assured Kanchha's father. 'Don't worry, Ba. The army can't just abduct people.'

In the following weeks, Rajan devoted himself to Kanchha's case, taking days off from work to help his lawyer friend prepare the habeas corpus writ. Each time he and Prema went to the Maya Lodge, he would update her on the latest. The lawyer had filed the habeas corpus writ, but so slow were the courts it would be months before the case would be heard, he told her. In the meanwhile the lawyer was pursuing clues as to the boy's whereabouts. A high-ranking police officer had assured Rajan that Kanchha was being held in the district jail; though when the lawyer inspected the jail, he did not find the boy. Then a man who had been released from army custody claimed to have seen a boy fitting Kanchha's description in the barracks. The lawyer had gone to meet the major who headed the barracks; but the major had insisted they were not holding the boy.

'Even if he were a Maoist, they have to give him due process,' Rajan would say to Prema. 'Even in wartime, there are rules of engagement. You can't do just anything. This is about the rule of law.'

This work aroused in him none of the frustration that his work for the organization did. Dissatisfied with the lawyer's progress, he began to lobby national and international human rights organizations in the capital. First he informed the International Committee of the Red Cross about Kanchha's disappearance. Then he lobbied Amnesty International which appealed for the boy's release. Officials at the Bar Association in the capital promised to follow up. Rajan was triumphant when Human Rights Watch mentioned Suk Bahadur Ale in one of their reports. 'He's in the barracks, I know it,' Rajan would say. 'He's here in this town. Right *here*.'

But all he had were rumours, some harrowing. A cleaner at

the barracks told the lawyer, one day, that inmates were tortured as a matter of course. Another day, Rajan heard that two soldiers had killed Kanchha while interrogating him and had buried him in a mass grave behind the barracks. The next week he heard that no, the boy was still alive. Nothing could be verified. All Rajan had was his own stubborn reasoning: 'How can they just make him disappear?'

They just could. Two months on, there was no news of the boy.

A Place Called Los Angeles

~

Prema was convinced the war would escalate from here on. The Maoists would not give up, and neither would the king and the army; and people who had nothing to do with either side would get drawn in. Should she not leave? This shabby, Third World country. Having received a chance— Having won a lottery. Was this not an opportunity to keep progressing? America was rich, it was—proper, solid. But wasn't it also—an agent of corporate capitalist expansionism? What would she do there? What would she do here, though? What if the army were to return to the hill bazaar? She recalled, with revulsion, the soldier who had asked her for identification. Or— What if the Maoists were to come here, as they had to her birth village? She kept feeling a shivering in the marrow.

America. Nepal. America. Nepal.

Both options felt wrong. Yet she had to make a choice, so choose she did. With the telephone lines down in the hill bazaar, she had to go more frequently to the town at the base of the hills to communicate with the head office. As soon as she received notification of her interview date, she telephoned the embassy. An official there, a woman this time, reminded her to bring cash to pay the application fee. As an afterthought the woman added, 'Where are you going to live? Do you have family or friends there? Have you thought about where to go when you land? Have you found a job for yourself?'

She turned to Rajan for help. And he helped her leave. It turned out that he knew a middleman with family members in America. 'He's not— I quit the Party because of people like him,' he explained to her. 'So much of politics revolved around greasing the right middleman. This man isn't— I don't like him,' he said, 'but he'll do anything for a cut.'

The middleman lived in the town at the base of the hills, in a cement bungalow fortified by high brick walls. Prema took along a large sum of cash when they went to visit. Past the front gate, a Tibetan mastiff lunged fiercely on its leash as they entered. They waited by the gate till a servant girl came and led them in.

They found the middleman in his bedroom watching television. When he saw Rajan he broke into a leer: 'Bastard dog,' he said, pushing himself up off the bed, 'all these years you've been too busy to stop by for a cup of tea?'

Rajan laughed in a game manner. 'I figured you were busy building your fortune, Harihar-dai. I didn't want to get in the way.'

They shook hands familiarly, clapping each other on the back.

'Sit, sit,' the middleman said. He was a thickset man with a watchful manner. He looked uneasy even when smiling. To Rajan he said, 'You think I don't know where you've been— lining your pockets with a fat salary! Poverty alleviation!' He snorted. 'How much do you earn in that NGO, eh?'

'Much less than you do, Harihar-dai.'

'Tell me!'

'It would only embarrass me to tell.'

Leering, the middleman turned to Prema. 'Forgive us, Sister. This one and I, we've known each other since we were—how to say this—in our underwear, as children. Before he became too big for the Party!'

'It's the Party that became too big for me,' Rajan said.

'Bastard dog!'

The television remained on to a concert of some kind. The servant girl brought in tea. Then Rajan got to the point: 'My friend here,' he said, 'won the green-card lottery. She needs a place to live, Harihar-dai. She needs a job in America.'

'You won the green-card lottery?' The middleman raised his brow. 'I knew a man who applied nine years and never won!'

'She needs your help,' Rajan said.

'New York, New York!' the middleman said. 'I have a friend there, a lady professor. Laura? Laurie? Dermott, from New York. She was doing her PhD on something. Marriage? Or death rituals.' He sneered: 'She fell in love with the District Education Officer, a married man! A girl with yellow eyes like a cat's. Here.' He got up, and from a high shelf took down a shoebox. 'Look in here, Sister.' He handed the box to Prema. 'There should be a postcard from her in there.'

Then he sat back down on the bed, and returned to needling Rajan about poverty alleviation.

The shoebox was full of postcards. Prema flipped through them, some crisp, most soft with age: postcards of faded seascapes, houses on stilts, monks, mountains, blue skies. Switzerland, the Caribbean, India, Fiji, Taiwan, Korea, Spain, New Zealand. On the television screen a woman stopped singing, to thunderous applause. Then a man took the stage. His name flashed on: Clint Black.

Eventually Prema found the postcard: a desert at twilight, cacti against a greenish-blue sky. On the back it said: *Dear Harihar, I'm back home but already want to return! How beautiful your mountains are! And the Nepalese people are so special. I will be back! Love and peace, Lauren*

'It doesn't have an address or telephone number,' Prema remarked.

'Eh, doesn't it?' The middleman reached over and took the card from her. 'You're right,' he said. 'Well, write down the name in any case. Once you get to America you can look her up in the telephone directory and ask her for help. It's incredible, they have directories in every telephone booth in America,' he said. 'I was there, once, in New York, not exactly New York but New Jersey, which is the same-same. I was there five years ago.'

Rajan and Prema exchanged glances. He spoke for her: 'We were hoping you could arrange something more concrete, Harihar-dai. A place she can live, and some work. My friend isn't rich,' he added, 'but this is important.'

'Eh.' The middleman gave Prema a swift, appraising glance. 'In that case I have a nephew, an American citizen. A smart boy, knows everything about the country, he's helped many compatriots resettle. He can set you up with a place to live, and a job.'

'How much would it cost?' Prema asked.

'I'll tell him it's for a friend.'

'How much?'

'For a close friend…fifty thousand up front, and a cut of your salary once you're there.'

She took out her cash and counted out fifty thousand.

The middleman pocketed it swiftly. 'I'll call him tonight,' he said. 'He'll get on the case at once—I'll tell him to expect your call, too. Let me get his address and number.' He went to another room and brought back a chit of paper. On it was scribbled: Narahari Bohora, 4592 Bluefield Ave, La Mirada 90638. Telephone: (562) 579-3985.

'Where is this?' Prema asked.

'In a place called Los Angeles.'

She was not quite sure where that was.

The middleman and Rajan returned to bantering. A pageant of advertisements flashed on the television screen. Prema watched, thinking—Los Angeles—till she noticed that the conversation had grown quite intent.

'We just want to know is if he's all right,' Rajan was saying. 'There have been so many rumours, his family is in despair.'

'A Gurkha soldier's son, eh? I'll see what I can do.'

'We think he's in the barracks.'

'A Maoist?'

'He's just fourteen.'

'Children get fanciful—'

'We just want to know where he is.'

Afterwards, the middleman escorted them out past the mastiff. He assured Prema that his nephew would start on her case at once. Then he shook hands with Rajan: 'I'll get back about the other matter.'

Once the arrangements were made, Prema no longer wanted to stay on in the hill bazaar. One day she stole away without telling anyone. She felt bad leaving. She didn't know why. Four months after his abduction, Kanchha was still missing. The cybercafe was still shuttered close, the telephone lines had not been restored. There was no end in sight to the war. It felt like she was abandoning everyone, to secure her own future. Yet that was what she did.

A few days before her interview at the embassy, she packed some clothes, shoes and books into a suitcase. She also packed the ammonite and the binoculars. The rest of her belongings she stored in a box that the schoolteacher couple could later dispose of as they wanted. She did not tell them she was not coming back. The next morning, when she said goodbye to them, and to Trailokya and his family, they did not know it was for the last time.

Rajan walked with her to the Maya Lodge. Even he thought she was going to the capital for only a week or so. He thought she would be coming back. She could not bring herself to tell him otherwise; she could not bear to acknowledge the end of their attachment. Along the trail lined with crown-of-thorns they talked not about their feelings, but of humanitarian law and war crimes, international human rights charters. Perhaps there was not much to say in the end; or Prema did not know how to say it. In any case, once they got to the Maya Lodge, their time together was cut short by a rapping on the door of Prema's room.

It was the middleman. He looked at Prema, then, leering indecently, turned back to Rajan: 'Can we talk?'

They went out to the hallway.

When Rajan came back to the room he looked stricken.

'He said he'll find out where Kanchha is if his father pays him a hundred thousand,' he said. He groaned, putting his hands to his head. 'Motherfucking middlemen! I hate them, I hate these people—how can they profiteer off a case like this?'

They spent the rest of the evening debating whether or not Kanchha's father should pay the middleman.

After the lights were out Prema did ask Rajan, 'Will you visit me in the capital?'

In the dark he said, 'I'll have to see if I can get a few days' leave.'

In the dark she did not say: Come with me to America. Or: Ask me to stay here with you.

And he did not say: Stay here with me. Or: Ask me to come with you.

At the American embassy, she was interviewed by a Derek Bending, a doughy man whose words flowed out continuously, lilting and mellifluous but not always comprehensible. Right off, he pressed a calling card into her hand. 'Premma: mind if I call you Premma? I'm Derek Bending. That's capital d for Detroit, e for Easter, r for royalty, e for Easter, k for king, capital b for boy, e for Easter, n for Nantucket, d for dog, i for igloo, n for Nantucket and g for god. You can call me Derek.' He had a ponytail. Apologizing for some reason Prema could not grasp, he pored over her application: 'Uh-huh. All right.' His eyes were a bright blue, reflecting light with a sparkle, as off a sapphire. 'Uh-huh, uh-huh.' When he saw that she had said she was moving to Washington D.C., he said, 'White House, here I come!' Then: 'You like politics?' Then: 'I had the best sandwich in D.C. once, an avocado wrap, don't remember the name of the restaurant—near Dupont Circle—it was excellent.' Then he asked, 'Do you know how to drive? You should learn how to drive.' After reviewing all her documents—'Yup, yup'—Mr Derek Bending pronounced, 'Well, Premma, everything looks A-okay from this end. Would you like to complete the payment now?'

She paid the embassy just about what she had paid the middleman.

Then Mr Derek Bending walked her out to the embassy gates.

'Good luck, Premma.'

'Thank you, Mr—Derek.'

She checked into the Kathmandu Hotel and began to prepare for departure.

From the hotel's front lobby she telephoned the middleman's nephew in Bluefield Ave, La Mirada. A middleman like his uncle, he offered to make all necessary arrangements in return for a cut. 'I can pick you up at the airport at no cost,' he said, solicitous. 'Let me know once you have the flight details, Bahini. I'll come to the airport to meet you.'

She sent a resignation letter to the head office.

She sent an email to Trailokya, telling him she would not be returning.

She sent a farewell letter to the schoolteacher couple, the remaining rent tucked inside, in cash.

She wrote an email to Rajan, telling him she was leaving for good.

Then she telephoned her birth village and asked the operator to fetch her father.

She hung up and waited.

When she called back in half an hour, he was waiting for her call.

She said: 'Ba, I'm going to America.'

'When will you come back, Chhori?' he asked, his voice soft and gravelly on the line.

'I'm going to live there, Ba.'

'And when will you come back?' he asked, uncomprehending.

'No,' she said. 'I'm going to live there. Forever.'

There was a pause.

'Do you know anyone there?' he asked.

'A friend is making arrangements.'

'Will you not come here to bid farewell?' he asked.

'Shall I come?'

There was another pause. 'It is not advisable,' he said at last.

On this side of the line she tried to stay strong: 'I'll keep sending money, Ba.'

'It's all right. It's all right,' he said gently. 'By your mother's blessings you're getting this chance to cross the seven seas,' he said. 'Use this opportunity well, Chhori. I know you will. You always do. The important thing is to take care of your health, to eat well, get enough sleep.' Then he said what he always said when they talked on the telephone: 'You will progress, Chhori, I know you will. By your mother's blessings you will lead the life she could not have. You will lead a complete life.'

The visa came through in two weeks, but Prema spent several more weeks in limbo in the capital waiting for an affordable airplane ticket. One day she went to the British Council to enrol in an advanced English-language class, but the deadline had passed, so she enrolled, instead, in classes at the Excellence Language Institute. She dropped out when she learned that the language teachers were no more fluent than she. Heeding Derek

Bending's words she took a few driving lessons, but she stopped when she found out that they drove on the other side of the road in America. Should she really go? Some days she was paralysed by doubt. She would sit by the window in her room at the Kathmandu Hotel, fingering her mother's ammonite. When she felt stronger she would walk through the tourist district picking out Americans from the trekkers who thronged the streets. At the bookstalls she read whatever she could find on the United States: the people and culture, the structure of government, history. In a cybercafe she discovered *Los Angeles Times* online.

Rajan never visited her. After he got her email he telephoned. 'I'll feel alone once you're gone,' he said, as though she were not already gone from his life. He confused her. Or their attachment confused her. For a while they telephoned every week. He would tell her about developments in Kanchha's case. The boy's father had decided not to pay the middleman. The boy's whereabouts were still unknown. They thought he was still alive, but they could not be sure. Prema would listen to all this, shuddering. 'Tell me if you find out anything more,' she would say; and he would promise, 'I will. I'll definitely let you know.'

But as the days passed it grew painful to draw out their separation. They were supposed to talk one day, and neither called. A week passed, then another. They exchanged a few emails but never spoke again.

When her ticket came through Prema again telephoned the middleman's nephew in Bluefield Ave, La Mirada, and gave him her arrival date and flight number.

'I'll be there to meet you, Bahini,' he assured her.

On the appointed day she took the flight to Los Angeles.

LA. She still thought of it as America. Throughout the flight she looked out at the sky. Three hours to Bangkok, and fourteen more to Los Angeles. In transit at the Bangkok airport, she heard two compatriots speaking in Nepali, the language of her sorrows. She rushed away from them, down the white halls, past the gates for Osaka, Dubai, Paris, Ankara, Melbourne, Amsterdam. She took the flight to Los Angeles. She was left to the world.

Twenty-Six

~

'Hey Prema, know what I had for dinner last night?' Luis asked the next time they met at Meadowvale. 'Dull-bath. A kind of Nepalese, I mean, Nepali, food.'

'Daal-bhat?' she asked, surprised.

'It was great!' He grinned. 'At a restaurant in Mar Vista called the Katmandu Kitchen. Know it?'

'No.'

'Know where Venice meets Overland?'

'No.'

'You should— Hey, maybe we could go there sometime,' he said.

Without quite meaning to, she bridled.

He immediately retreated. 'Though I bet you eat dull-bath all the time, huh.'

'No,' she said, trying to be nice. 'I do not cook so much.'

'You don't like it?' he asked.

'I do,' she said. 'Just—the ingredients. I don't know where to buy them.'

'I liked it a lot,' he said. 'There was also—tur-curry?'

'Tarkaari. Vegetables.'

'It was great. Really great.'

'That is nice,' she said.

'Yeah.'

'Nice.'

'Yeah.'

Her birthday came that summer. Twenty-six: the age her mother had lived to be. Impossible not to dwell on this; but Prema trained her attention on the dissimilarities in their lives. That Saturday, she went to the beach by Esther's house to spend the day there the way Americans did. She brought along her binoculars. The shore was cool and misty in the summertime gloom. Shoeless, she walked along the sand to the waterline, where the surf, receding, left lush, lacy tendrils of foam. She didn't own a swimsuit and didn't know how to swim, but she stood within the reach of the water and observed the crests rising, curling, booming, crashing.

Then she urged herself to go farther. Heading north, she took the path past the boat harbour, past the library where she got Esther's large-print romances, and past glassy high-rises. Condos. She walked till she eventually reached a tourist beach.

The coastline here was jammed with parking lots, shops and restaurants, all the way to the horizon. There was a crush of people looking ebullient for no particular reason. 'It was a smart investment,' she heard one woman saying to another. 'How's it hangin', dude?' a man called out. A gang of teenagers rushed past her, and a bicyclist with Rastafarian braids sailed by, shouting into his mobile telephone: 'Just tell 'em you changed your mind!'

At the waterline, she trained her binoculars north, and in the haze saw a Ferris wheel. Santa Monica. Above the water, gulls and terns were hovering and diving for fish. Sardines? Anchovies? Fishermen, dark and huddled, were waiting for a bite on a pier. Was it safe to eat the fish caught in these waters? A wave crashed down not far from where she was standing. Receding, it left behind a frond of seaweed, glass-green with sinewy bulbs. She picked it up. It was slippery and cool, clean, a translucent bottle green. She put it into her pocket.

At home that evening, she examined the seaweed, now dry and rubbery. In her first year in America, Prema had bought a field guide at a Salvadorian street fair. She consulted it now, and discovered that the seaweed was a sea palm. Sea palm. Look. She had come from the mountains, all the way to the ocean. From Nepal to America. A hill bazaar to a metropolis of millions. Her mother's life to hers. A frond of sea palm in her hands.

The following day, Prema returned to the tourist beach, determined to go even farther. At one of the stalls, she bought a red bikini for $24.99, and flip-flops for $4.47. She changed into it at a public toilet—restroom—examining, in the mirrors by the washstands, the way the bikini curved over her breasts and back.

Outside, she walked to the water and waded into a swelling wave, the foam fizzling at her calves. Was it safe? She waded out, sucking in her breath involuntarily as the chill slapped her thighs. Then a wave surged up. She jumped its foamy crest, checking afterwards to see if the bikini had stayed in place. It had. A current drew her out as the wave receded, but then another wave surged toward her, sending her back inshore. She found her footing again. A young couple were jumping the crests nearby. Mimicking them she jumped as the water level rose; then she jumped again when it rose again. She did this successfully awhile, but then a massive wave swelled up without warning and with a force she had not anticipated knocked her sideways and dragged her roughly over the sand.

Sputtering, blinded by saltwater, she scrambled to her feet as the wave receded, just as another wave swelled forward. She dodged that and the next few waves, finally regaining her balance. And slowly, slowly, she began to feel at ease in the water.

The next time at Meadowvale, she went to Luis's desk: 'Do you know what I did?'

He looked up from his paperwork. 'Oh, hey, Prema. Let me guess. You cooked dull-bath and ate it all by yourself.'

She laughed. 'No. I went into the ocean.'

'Yeah, the water's getting warm, isn't it? I was out in Redondo a few weeks ago.'

'It was my first time,' she said, eager to confess this.

'You're putting me on. You like it?'

'I thought I might drown, but I did not.'

'Yeah, it's different from swimming in a pool. People fight the currents, wear themselves out. You have to work with the waves.'

'I cannot swim in a pool, even.'

'What, no swimming pools in Nepal? But then, you have the himmels.'

'Always your himals.'

He laughed. 'It bugs you, doesn't it? It bugs you. You think: why is this guy going on about something he doesn't know—'

'I also do not know about the ocean.'

'You been in LA long, Prema?'

'Three years.'

'Huh. And this was your first time in the water?'

'I liked it.'

'Well, you're a real Angeleno now.'

And something changed between them. They stopped talking only on his terms, maybe, or she extended herself to him. Or they finally understood, a bit, where the other was coming from. When they met every two weeks they would pick up on their conversations as though so many days had not passed in between.

'You are a student of that guru?' Prema asked once, pointing at the locket on Luis's bracelet.

He shook off the bracelet and examined the guru on the locket. 'Nah. They were handing it out on the street and I thought the guru looked cool, you know—all wizened and wrinkly, like Yoda.'

'Does yoga really give you wrinkles? Do you know, that guru is a murderer?'

'You're putting me on.'

She told him about the murder case and his imprisonment. Then he explained to her who Yoda was.

Two weeks later, in the cafeteria over lunch with Esther and her friend Donald, Luis showed Prema the bracelet, free of the locket: 'Look, no killer guru.'

She told him that when the mists cleared, she could see Mount Everest from her birth village: 'But there was always mist.'

He told her he had grown up in San Diego, a—his term—beach bum. 'Always goofing off at Windansea, playing hooky with my stepbrother. I can't even imagine not being able to swim,' he said. 'Know what you should do? Take swimming lessons at the Y.'

The next time they met he asked, 'So did you live in the same village all your life?'

She told him she had gone to college in the capital, and then gone to work across the country, in a hill bazaar.

'Could you see the himmels from there too?'

'No, just the foothills—mountains.'

'Boy, you must miss the mountains, here.'

'I live on a hill, not so far from downtown.'

'Oh, right. So you come in on the one-ten in the morning?'

'I take the number thirty-three.'

'The what?'

'The number thirty-three.'

'The *bus*?'

'I do not know how to drive,' she explained.

'Huh.' He said, 'Yeah, I guess in Nepal— Wow. The bus. That's new.'

Later, Luis told Prema that after she had turned down his invitation to the Katmandu Kitchen, he had figured that she wasn't, as he put it, looking. And he had his own reasons to hesitate. He had only just got through with a divorce. And he felt that most girls—his term—weren't gone on a guy with so much baggage—also his term for his daughter, July.

'July?'

'The month she was born. Tina—my ex—thought it was pretty.'

Yet as their friendship progressed, their conversations grew more playful.

'What is the why?' Prema asked him one week.

'The what?'

'You said I should take swimming classes at the why.'

'You mean the Y.'

The next time, she asked, 'What do you mean I am putting you on when you say I am putting you on?'

They laughed a lot in each other's company. Maybe they came to each other smiling.

They soon began to confide in each other. One day, visibly frustrated—though about what, he did not say—Luis said, 'Don't you find all this—empty? Like all we Americans ever do is work and shop and pay taxes and die?'

'It is the same everywhere, no?' Prema said.

'Is it? Maybe that's the whole point. The Buddhists say it's all about emptiness.'

'You are Buddhist too, now?'

'No, no,' he said. 'I'm not Buddhist. I'm—nothing. General Administrator.' He laughed. 'It's not like anyone grows up wanting to be an administrator, right? It just works out that way. Look, Prema: I work for a company that makes a profit off old folks. All those forms on my desk? They're about which regulations to meet, how to qualify for payment schemes. It's all—empty.' He said, 'Meaningless.' He said, 'At least in your work, you're actually helping a real live person, you know. You like working for Mrs King?'

'She is interesting.'

'This the kind of work you did back home?'

'I was a forester.'

'What, like Smokey Bear?'

'I studied forestry in college,' she explained.

'Huh.' He said, 'Hey, you know my father was Guatemalan? You think you're the only multicultural one here?' He smiled. 'Dad was born in Guatemala. He came to America when he was young. Before I was born.' Slyly, he added, 'Way, way before you were born.'

She smiled. 'I am twenty-six years old.'

'Well, I'm over the hill—thirty-three! July's already seven. She lives with my ex, out in the valley.'

'Valley?'

He gave her a look. 'How long did you say you've lived in LA?'

'Three years.'

'Jesus. Where have you been?'

The Reyes City Tour

~

She asked him out in the end. Her swim in the ocean had changed her somehow. For the first time in America she was...happy. She felt it was possible to reinvent herself. Every morning now, leaving the hot, stifled inland for the coast, she kept wanting to go farther.

And why not? One afternoon at the beach, she watched the two bikini-clad teenagers doing gymnastics: the blonde did a handstand, and then the brunette imitated her. They made it look so easy.

Beside her, Esther and Sam were talking in their usual manner: 'Build on the coast, build in the hills, build in the plains,' Sam was saying, 'so this company wants to build on the wetlands, and the city says go right ahead!' Esther cut in with: 'We met him at a gala dinner.' Sam continued: 'They tried to stop it, doll, the fellow who played the president, Martin Sheen, and all the hotshot Hollywood actors. Ed Asner: Lou.' 'I was talking about Casper Weinberger!' 'But the developers got a piece. Have you seen the condos, doll? Out by Loyola Marymount?'

During a lull in their conversation, Prema asked Sam: 'Where is the wetlands?'

He waved a beer-filled cup inland. 'That-a-way, doll.'

'Did you know?' Prema asked Luis the next time they met at Meadowvale. 'There is a wetlands near the international airport.'

'Yeah, Ballona, out on Jefferson.'

'Let us go there sometime.'

He raised an eyebrow. 'You asking me on a date?'

All of a sudden the heat rose to Prema's face. She didn't know where to look: at Luis, at the ceiling, at the floor.

He smiled. 'How's this Saturday? You free for lunch? Where do you live? I'll swing by and pick you up.'

Perhaps there is, in every friendship, a threshold past which everything aids seduction. With Rajan, this had happened at a meeting in the head office, over a tea break. He had made a few wry jokes about development, and after that, he and Prema had exchanged glances at every grand claim made by a colleague. After that, he had begun to come by the hill bazaar to meet her; and one day, he had suggested they go to the town at the base of the hills. That night they had stayed together at the Maya Lodge. With the only other man Prema had had sex with, Andy, there had been no seduction at all. Now here was Luis Reyes. Before asking him out, Prema had not really looked at him, she had not really seen him; but now she found herself thinking of his face. His smile. His liquid, honey-brown eyes. Astonished by the reawakening of her desire. Moving her hands as his.

The wetlands turned out to be a small expanse of cattails and rushes and—where it was dry—coastal scrub, hemmed in by roads and houses. After picking her up, Luis drove to Esther's neighbourhood, and parked by the curb. 'Here we are.'

The wetlands lay beyond a wooden fence, and a signboard prohibiting entry. They stood by the fence in the mild, honeyed breeze, which carried the scent of Luis's cologne, citrus and mint, to Prema.

She had brought along her binoculars and field guide. Nearby, two waterbirds were dipping their heads in a dark reflective pool. The waterbirds were dark on top, with long, white throats, red eyes, and orange beaks. Western grebes.

Luis pointed at a smaller waterbird by a clump of tules. 'Loons.'

Within minutes they sighted bushtits flitting through the scrubs, a loggerhead shrike perched on a reed, two snowy egrets wading in a creek, a black phoebe and a meadowlark, darting. 'I've never really done any birdwatching before,' Luis admitted. Prema said, 'Me not so much either.' At one point Luis sighted a great blue heron: tall, with a black-and-silver crown, white plumes spiking out the chest, and wings of shimmering grey. It was standing at the edge of the pool hunting for fish. So elegant a bird. Prema searched for the term: 'Stalking.'

'Isn't that just so cool.'

Then they sat in the car with the windows down and ate submarine sandwiches that Luis had picked up on the way. He told her about a hike that he and his ex-wife had taken many years ago, with their daughter. 'A complete disaster! Tina had seen this television show about a cougar that had snatched a little kid in Topanga, and she was terrified the whole time. Plus we got lost. But there had been a brushfire the year before, and the seeds of this plant—Indian paintbrush?—had all cracked open. There were these amazing flowers, all red. Just out of this world.'

She asked him if he had ever been to his father's land.

'Nah. I'd love to go sometime. But then, there are lots of other places I want to go, you know? Like Mount Everest. You ever think of going back, Prema?'

'No.'

'Dad never went back either. He died nine years ago of pancreatic cancer. Both your parents alive, Prema?'

'My father is.'

'My mom, Peggy, lives in San Diego with my stepdad. I've got a stepbrother in Arizona. You stay in touch with your dad much?'

'Not so much.'

'Why did you come anyway? To America, I mean.'

Luis had never heard of the green-card lottery. 'Whoa, whoa,' he said when she told him. 'Don't tell me our government lottoes off green cards! Holy sh—' He raised his brows. 'So you came only because you hit the jackpot?'

'Yes.'

'Huh. And you don't want to go back, even for a visit?'

'No.'

'Is it because of the war?'

'No,' she said. Then, 'Maybe.' Then, 'No.'

'I googled it, it sounds bad, huh. Your dad safe?'

She shrugged. 'As safe as everyone else.'

'I'm sorry,' he said. 'That must be real heavy.'

She waited for the topic to pass.

In a while they went back out of the car and stood at the fence, looking in at the wilderness. 'Thank you for bringing me here,' she said.

'Hey. Glad you asked me out.'

Their eyes met, and all of a sudden the heat rose to her face. 'Early morning and late afternoon are the best times for bird-watching,' she said, turning away to hide her blush.

He smiled. 'Hand me the binoculars? That great blue heron's still there.'

His arm brushed against hers, shooting desire through her entire body.

At three he drove her back to her house on the dry, grassy hill. He didn't try to kiss her. He didn't even reach for her hand. He just said, 'I really enjoyed that.'

'Yes,' she said.

'Do that again sometime?'

'Yes.'

'See you next Tuesday at Meadowvale?'

'Yes.'

Later, she could not say that the hum of air conditioning in Meadovwale's lobby, the fluorescent lighting, the multicoloured vinyl sofas and the classical music wafting out of concealed speakers did not add to her attraction to Luis. The absence of dust in his world. His ease with where he was. His crisp white shirt and brown slacks, the citrus and mint of his cologne. His being so—American. It all mingled in.

The following Tuesday they sat in the lobby and flirted.

'Hey, I was thinking,' he said. 'If you're up for it, I could give you the Reyes city tour of el Pueblo de Nuestra Señora la Reina de los Angeles.'

'But is it expensive?' she said brazenly.

'Oh, we could come up with an arrangement.'

She blushed, wishing she would not blush so in his presence.

He smiled. 'July's with me this weekend, but if you're free Thursday evening I'll take you to Griffith Park.'

'Yes.'

All Thursday her mind thrummed; the whole world sparkled. That afternoon, at the beach, as Esther gossiped about a Sally Macrae, about a barber who used to cut Tim's hair, about a UN official from Santiago who had tried to kiss her, Prema closed her eyes, took in the boom of the ocean, and felt intensely alive.

At the end of the workday, she changed into an indigo dress that she had bought, along with the field guide, at a Salvadorian street fair in her first year in America. She thought of it as her Bollywood-heroine dress: the neckline flared at the chest and the skirt caught at the hips.

'Going out for dinner, dear?' Esther asked when she saw her dressed up. 'Do you have a date with a fella?'

'Yes, Esther.'

'Is he a decent fella?'

'I think so.'

'Be careful, dear. Elizabeth Beard's daughter was dating a fella, seemed like a gentleman, but turned out to have a record. Embezzlement of funds!' She cast a cool eye over Prema's neckline. 'Young people these days fling themselves at each other. You must make the fella wait, dear.'

But when the doorbell rang and Luis was there, in jeans and a smart red sport shirt, Prema was ready for anything.

He gave her a chaste hug. 'You look great.'

'You also.'

'That's a great dress.'

'You like it?'

'Yeah!'

She felt snug and insulated in his car. He put on some jaunty rock music as he drove. 'You ready for the tour?' Nearing the freeway, he pointed at a low, glass office building. 'See that place? I worked there for two years. Max Dental. My first job after college.'

'What kind of tour is this?'

He smiled. 'Patience, patience.'

In a while he turned on to a road that snaked up a hill, to a ridge pocked with drills. Drills? 'Oil!' Prema cried. 'Those are for oil! No?'

Luis smiled at her surprise. 'Stick with the Reyes city tour, señorita, you'll see a thing or two.'

He drove confidently on the freeway, skirting downtown. Prema—who knew the metropolis only along the bus routes—could not tell where they were after a while. At one point he pulled into a petrol pump—a gas station—to fill the car. Super unleaded. He hopped back in and revved the engine, merging smoothly into the oncoming traffic. 'A Hummer,' he said of a tank ahead. 'You know what kind of mileage? My Saturn isn't the coolest car, but it gives me twenty-nine miles to the gallon.'

Then he turned up a hill and took a winding road to a tree-covered ridge. They parked and got out to the scent of peppery woods. Jeffrey pines. Coastal sage. Chaparral.

'Welcome to Griffith Park,' he said. 'They're not the himmels, but they're all we've got.'

Before them, the Hollywood sign floated above the smog. All around lay low hills. Mountains, the Americans called them. They looked majestic from this vantage point. She saw, for the first time, the beauty of this land. The leaves in the forest were crackling dry in this season. Gnats danced around them in the sunlight. Somewhere, a raven cawed. A lizard skittered off a rock, into an elderberry shrub.

'Look,' Luis said.

Beyond the ridge: the metropolis, a patchwork of broken grids and freeways. Prema recognized the skyscrapers downtown and the dry, grassy hill that she lived on. Luis pointed out his neighbourhood, beyond, but she couldn't quite make it out in the smog. Neither could she recognize Little Nepal, where she had spent her first year in America.

They stood side by side, looking out at the view till sunset. Then Luis drove them back down the hill to a diner in a neighbourhood that consisted entirely of shops and restaurants.

Over hamburgers and beer he asked about her life back home. She hardly knew where to begin. She told him a bit about her studies and the work she had done in the hill bazaar.

'You sound real serious, even as a kid,' he said. 'Focused.'

'You were not?'

He had partied through college, drinking, doing dope—marijuana—and later, taking something called acid. 'Messing around, you know.' He had quit when he had met his ex-wife. Tina was a yoga instructor. 'She got me into meditation, cleaned me up.'

'Was it difficult to get divorced?'

'Yeah, a bit.' He grimaced. 'Tina and I were having some problems, nothing serious, then she went and fell for this—dork. Our meditation guru, actually! He was also married—even had a teenage daughter.' He laughed. 'Some guru!'

'I think these gurus are like that,' Prema said.

'She's married to him now—they just bought a house, too. How about you?' he said. 'You ever been serious about anyone?'

'In Nepal I had a—boyfriend,' she said, for lack of a more appropriate term for Rajan.

'You loved him?'

She had never talked to a man she liked about a man she had loved. 'We were close,' she said.

'So what happened?'

'I came here.'

'You still in touch?'

'No.'

'Hey.' He reached over for her hand, setting her heart racing. 'I hope you don't mind my asking all these personal questions.'

'No,' she murmured.

He looked at her, opening his mouth to say something. Then he stopped. Then he said, 'So, you like me at all? 'Cause I really like you.'

To her immense embarrassment, she blushed fiercely. 'You like me or you like that I am from Nepal?' she joked.

'You're so—different—from any girl I've known,' he said. 'Plus you're pretty damn hot.'

Her blush only deepened. 'I like you too,' she mumbled. Then, meeting his eyes, she decided to go farther. 'I also think you are hot.'

His eyes lit up, and he leaned over and kissed her.

Nothing was enough for her after that, she needed Luis, only he would do. Or was it sex? On their next date he invited her over to his place, and she tingled for him during the entire drive there. She could not help wondering how he would be in bed. She knew from magazines and the Internet that Rajan and she had not done all the things that Americans did. From Andy she had learnt nothing. Luis, Luis. Her blood was on fire.

He drove south, through a neighbourhood of pretty Spanish-style bungalows: 'Manhattan Beach. Where I'm going to live in my next life.' His own neighbourhood was inland, by a plaza, where all the buildings were identical, as on a toy street. His flat was in one of these buildings. It was hard to miss the dancing Shiva in the living room, a bronze bracketed by small black speakers. Otherwise there was just a sofa, a coffee table, a television set. 'It's, um, a bit recently-divorced,' he said.

The kitchen was also very tidy. 'Your flat is always so neat?' she teased him as he made a pot of coffee, decaffeinated.

'Flat.' He laughed. 'Here we call it apartment. The truth? I was a bit of a slob before Tina. You know what housebroken means? Marriage will do that to you. It got me cooking, too. You cook much, Prema?'

'A little.'

'Dull-bath?'

'Also that.'

When the coffee was made, they went to the living room, and talked about nothing much—did they believe in god? He did, she didn't, but did it matter?—that sort of thing. They sat on opposite ends of the sofa at first. When he got up to put on a CD, she got up to look at the dancing Shiva. When they sat back down, they were closer. Then he moved to her.

He kissed her. 'Is this okay?'

She followed the trail of his breath.

They kissed again, softly—lips, neck, earlobes, cheek, lips—till, unable to hold back, Prema pressed against him, more and more urgently, to get what she wanted: underneath his shirt, his torso.

His thighs, shapely in his jeans.

He pulled her to him, and it felt so good, and somehow, she was soon on his lap, straddling him as he worked off her shirt. *I want him.*

He drew back, flushed. 'You want to—? Shall we go to the bedroom?'

She really, really, really wanted to go farther. 'Please?' she said, 'I want you to teach— I do not know so many things.'

'You're not—?' He sat up, suddenly serious. 'Have you ever—?' Gingerly: 'Are you telling me you're a virgin?'

'Oh.' Was it good or bad, how she was? She said, 'No.'

'Oh, thank goodness!' He put a hand to his heart. 'Jesus, you had me worried!' He laughed in relief. Then he asked, 'So what do you want me to teach you?'

She was too shy to tell him, so she showed him instead. She undid his shirt and slowly traced the galaxy of spots and freckles on his chest, his nipples the colour of coffee. The bracelet on his wrist like a chain. Holding him down by it she kissed him on the neck, taking in a soft trembling in his veins. That trembling aroused her: she wanted him to tremble for her. 'Tell me if you want to stop,' he said; but all she could whisper was: 'Please.'

'Please what?'

She knelt, kissing him, making him sigh. She tasted him where he was tender and ran her tongue along his veins, taking him in. 'Teach me.'

'Oh, god. Oh god, oh god.'

Then in a while he drew her up and she was all his to have.

'Please,' she gasped.

'Please what?'

'Please.'

'Please what?' He put his lips there—right there—causing waves of pleasure, till, to her surprise, she came with a cry.

Then he took out a condom from a side table. When he entered her it felt as though this was what she was made for. First he made her lie on the sofa, and then he made her kneel to give him his satisfaction. All her thoughts were obliterated: all she could do was shiver. She heard a moan—him? her?—and when he came she felt him pulsing through the latex.

Afterwards they lay in each other's arms, stunned by pleasure.

He put a hand to her face, tenderly. 'Was it okay? I should have taken you to the bedroom. Was it all right?'

She murmured: 'Mmm.'

'Man, you're hot,' he said.

'Oh, god,' she murmured.

'*Now* you believe in god?'

In a while he got up and went, naked, to the bathroom. He came out, still naked, and sat on the sofa, looking at her.

'You bought that condom for me?' she teased him. 'Or you already had it?'

'I'm not telling!' He laughed. Then, 'I bought a pack this morning when I went grocery shopping.' He joked: 'Hey, there's plenty more where that came from—' Then he said, 'You need to go home tonight? 'Cause you could stay if you wanted.'

It was Saturday the next day. 'Can I stay?' Prema asked, more to herself than to him.

'There's a great place in the plaza we could have pancakes.'

They went to his bedroom and lay side by side on his bed, talking, tracing each other's warm, enjoyable shape, till their desire rose again. And again they made love, discovering their own bodies and the other's: the startling flares of pleasure, combustions, explosions.

Oh, god, Prema thought, opening again to Luis.

'Is this all right?' he whispered.

'Please. Please.'

'Please what?'

Please.

'Please what? Please what?'

Please give me this always, she thought. Luis's hair, damp with perspiration. His thighs, flexing and flexing. The power of his body rushing through her. Give me this. She gasped. This is all I'll ever want.

Arrival

~

Prema awakened to pleasure that autumn. The scorching inland heat, the wildfires in the hills, the breezes along the coast: everything kindled a blind lust in her. *I want him.* Luis, a reward for having left her past and reinvented herself. Or— Had she been so stupid? It was as if something so obvious, so self-evident, had been revealed to her so late. Sex. Had *this* not been the point of life all along? Her spirit effervesced, she felt speedy, propelled by joy. Luis was so free. He freed her. She had never in her life walked about naked, as an adult, the way she did in his flat. She had never played physically the way she did with him. Her whole being sizzled with satisfaction. He allowed her to learn about him, to put her lips there, to kiss, to lick, to feel him, to rub, to suck. To slide a hand there, feel, slip a finger in. To pull, to push, to hold, to release, to say, 'I like that,' 'More,' 'Again,' to moan, to squeal, to scream: everything. 'She likes it,' he would say, and she would blush. 'I like it,' she would murmur, and he would smile. The scent of milk, his skin, dizzied her. When they were apart the memory of his body shot through her, juddering: she was always aroused. And when they were together, he could make her want him just by looking at her. She felt Luis was taking her—not too late—to the tender, throbbing heart of life. To—as the Americans say—do it. Have sex. Make love. Get laid. Fuck. Fuck your brains out. Screw. Lick, kiss, suck. Come. Feel lush, fertile. Inextinguishable.

American man. Luis had drunk his first beer, a Corona, at fourteen. He had got a learner's permit at fifteen and a driver's licence on his sixteenth birthday. He had smoked marijuana the same year. He had lost his virginity in the back of his father's Ford to a girl in high school called Serenity White. He had bodysurfed almost every day till the age of eighteen. He had come to LA for college and stayed on. He and Tina had married after a year of their relationship, and she had immediately got pregnant. They were making a conscious attempt to remain friends after the divorce, though it was tough sometimes.

At the end of their dates, if Prema wasn't already at Luis's flat, they would go there to make love. His lips, delectable, the veins on his forearms like rivers she could swim in. The width of his shoulder blades narrowing to his hips, his muscles curving out again. She would trace his ribcage, feel the throbs at his pulse points, listen to his heartbeat. Begging, 'Please.' 'Oh, god,' he would say when she took control. Or he would take charge: 'I'm not done with you. Not yet. Not yet. Not. Yet.'

Till they were done.

'You are a Hindu sex god,' she teased him one night.

'It's you,' he laughed. 'I've never had this kind of sex before. Really.'

'No.'

'Really.'

But for Prema it was him. He initiated her into pleasure.

'What is that called?' she asked once, as he lay with his head between her thighs. 'Not— I know oral sex.'

'Eating,' he said. 'Eating out. Some people say eating at the y.'

'The same Y where they give swimming lessons?'

He laughed. 'Not that kind. What do you call it in Nepali?'

'People do not—' She said, 'You do not talk about it.'

'People do it but don't talk about it?'

'I do not know if people do it,' she confessed.

He said, 'But you've done this before. Or someone's done it to you.'

'No.'

'Well, consider this a complimentary part of the Reyes city tour.'

Prema could see that Luis enjoyed her company. He liked showing her around. On their dates, he took her to what he called his favourite joints—Thai, Mexican, Indian, Korean restaurants all over the metropolis. They went to the Cineplex with velveteen seats and popcorn-and-drink combos. They went to parlours packed with video games, pinball machines, shooting ranges, air hockey tables. They rode the Ferris wheel at Santa Monica, they went to theme parks and got headaches from going on too many rides. Prema had never realized, before, how much of an effort Americans put into amusing themselves. *This*, then, was America, she thought. She had reached it at last. She still found it strange at times. One evening, past a neighbourhood with a signpost 'Little El Salvador', they crossed over what looked like a culvert, embanked with cement. 'The LA River,' Luis said. 'Why cement a whole river?' Prema asked, and he told her about the justifications given and the scandals wrought: 'A lot of LA's history is tied up in the river.' Another day, he drove her through miles of low-income blocks. 'This is like a town near where I worked in Nepal,' she said, thinking of the town at the base of the hills. He laughed: 'Is it really?' 'Why in America is there poverty at all?' Prema asked, suddenly serious. 'Yeah!' he agreed; but he had no explanation. From there he took her across the freeway to see a famous theatre, a wax museum, an underwear store, a pavement with the names of famous film stars. 'Hollywood's not as glamorous as you'd think,' he said. But Prema was impressed later, when they drove through a hillside neighbourhood with high hedges offering glimpses of mansions: a column, an arch, a Greek statue.

At first she thought it was just a few mansions, but as they drove on she gaped at the wealth that unfolded.

'These folks here, they're the masters of the universe,' Luis said.

From there, he drove to a ridge top to show her the valley where his ex-wife and daughter lived. Then he drove back down the hill.

He drove so much: hours every day. He did not mind it. 'This is a drive-by city,' he would say. 'You gotta learn to drive if you're going to live in LA.' He called his car 'the Saturn', as though it were a pet with a proper name. There were papers strewn over the back seat of the Saturn, and T-shirts, a baseball cap, running shoes, a straw hat, flip-flops. There was a *Thomas Guide* in the glove compartment, but Luis rarely consulted it. When they made plans he would rehearse the routes out loud. 'If we want to get to Wilshire by eight, we need to zip up the four-oh-five and cut across the ten,' he would say. He was confident through blockages and diversions. 'All we have to do is hook up with the one-oh-five, then exit on to the seven-ten.'

In his car, when he was not listening to traffic reports, he would put on music. 'You know this?' Rock. Pop. Blues. Country. 'You like reggae?' he would ask, or, 'Celtic bands? Latin beats? Maybe you'd like punk,' he would say, or, 'How about alternative country? There's one thing you should know: Lyle Lovett *is* God. Or do you prefer hip hop? Calypso? African mixes? Try this,' he would say, and slip in a CD: songs about a rocket man, waiting for your man, the revolution starts, refugee this and refugee that, drunk at two, the man comes around, the wall closes in, and getting right with God.

Prema loved it all. Luis introduced her to television programmes about the mafia, doctors, lawyers, schoolteachers, policemen. He followed sports, too: American football, baseball, tennis, soccer, ice hockey. 'I watch so much TV,' he groaned one evening. 'You must think I'm so shallow.'

'You are exotic,' she said.

'*I'm* exotic?' He laughed. Then he said, 'You know what? I keep thinking—you're like this fragment from a faraway land that's come into my world. There's something so amazingly—different—about you.' He said, 'I mean, I've never been with anyone who isn't American, right? But I feel like I really *know* you. It feels like there's something...don't laugh, okay?'

'All right.'

'There's something so *elemental* about you.'

She laughed.

'I know, I know, it's corny. What I mean is there are so many—*cultural*—differences between us. But it's like there's no Nepal, no America. Just *us*, you know?'

She did not know. But she found him so endearing at that moment, she reached over and kissed him.

'Hey, Prema?' he said. 'You really like me?'

'Of course.'

'You don't think I'm—'

'What?'

'It's just— Sometimes I worry— Tina— But then— I guess I'm still kind of bruising from the divorce.' He took in a deep breath and changed the subject: 'So, tell me. What did you do for fun when you were a kid?'

She thought back to her childhood, to the few forms of entertainment that there had been. 'I played marbles,' she said.

'No kidding.'

She told him that when she was growing up there was no electricity in her village; there was no radio, no television, no diversion. 'But there was one girl in my school who had blue marbles,' she said, thinking back to her schooldays. 'Her uncle had brought them for her, from the capital. All the other girls wanted those marbles. We kept playing against her so that we could win one. Just one.' She laughed.

'You ever win one?'

'No.'

'No electricity, huh. God, I can't even imagine. See what I mean? That's so—*elemental*.'

Prema said, 'There is electricity now. There is even a telephone office.'

'Telephone office?'

'You call and ask the telephone operator to tell whoever you want to call to come later. Then you call again later.'

'Amazing,' he said. Then, 'Hey, if you ever want to use my cell, I don't know what the rates are to Nepal, but—'

'It is all right.'

He looked at her. 'Yeah. Family, huh? I don't call my mom

and stepdad much either, though they're just there.' He gestured south. 'I get it.'

How could he get it?

Or maybe he could.

On their next date he gave her a bag of aquamarine marbles. 'Saw it in a stall on Olvera, and I thought of those marbles you wanted as a kid,' he said. 'I thought—I know a girl who'd like a bag of marbles.'

They were having lunch at a restaurant downtown, a restaurant that revolved, offering a panoramic view of the metropolis.

The marbles were bigger and shinier than those from Prema's childhood. 'Thank you,' she said.

'My pleasure,' Luis said. 'Really. It is my pleasure. You know—' He looked into her eyes for a long time, meaningfully. 'I know there's lots of differences between us, but I think there's something special between us. I think we really complement each other. I mean, even though you're from such—another—world. And I— The differences aren't an obstacle, in fact they're— What I'm trying to say is—' He was getting flustered. 'I haven't felt this way since—' He took in a deep breath. 'I never thought I'd want to meet anyone again, after the divorce. I thought—who needs this, you know? I thought at most I'd date around a bit. But then— I'm falling for you pretty hard here, Prema. I just feel— I think— You make my world bigger,' he said. Then he blurted out, 'I love you.'

Nobody had ever said this to Prema before, this line from Hollywood, Bollywood cinema.

She tried out the sound of the words: 'I love you too.'

It came out odd: tinny. The words so slick from overuse that all meaning glanced off them.

But Luis did not seem to notice. 'Yeah?' he said, 'I really think I love you.'

'I love you,' Prema said again.

'I love you,' Luis said.

They kissed. And the kiss was reassuring.

Afterwards, driving her back home, Luis was happy. 'Hey, you ever been to Olvera?' he said. 'Wait, let's see if we can take it in.' Detouring, he drove her by the original settlement of Los Angeles, now redeveloped with shops and restaurants. 'Ain't no pueblo left here!' he said.

From there he took her on a spin—his words—to Dodger Stadium. Going for a spin meant driving just for fun. He sped along the freeway, putting on a CD with a song about wild horses. He sighed. 'Don't you just love the Stones?'

She said she didn't really know their music.

He gave her a look. 'You have *heard* of them, right?'

'The Rolling Stones?'

'Though I guess why should you have.'

He got off the freeway and looped around the exit ramp.

'I also know Nuclear Energy,' she said. 'They play a style of music called garage-house rock. And in Nepal I saw Clint Black once on television. I think he plays in the style called country.'

He laughed. 'So, what are Nepali songs like? Sing me one.' He turned off the CD player.

She sang a fragment of a mournful folk song, then broke off to the hum of the car engine. She said, 'It means it is raining and the woman's husband has gone away and she is in the pasture, alone. Now you sing.'

'Oh, no, no, no. We wouldn't want that.' Luis laughed.

They had reached the stadium. He said, 'Okay, here we are.

This, señorita, is a genuine American landmark.' He turned into a parking lot. 'The city built it when the Dodgers moved from Brooklyn. You know about the Dodgers? You gotta know about the Dodgers if you're going to be an Angeleno,' he said. 'There was some controversy about the stadium. The city moved lots of people out. You know Ry Cooder? He's, like, a communist, but I love his music. He made a CD about it. Here, I think I've got it.'

Slipping in the CD, he stopped by the exit of the parking lot. A bus stopped at the intersection, blocking the way. Luis idled, waiting for the bus to pass. In the Saturn, the singer began to croon about a poor man's Shangri-La. The aquamarine marbles Luis had given Prema lay on her lap, shimmering in the bag. Luis was so—kind. Prema looked over at him. He was looking out at the bus that was blocking the intersection. Following his gaze, Prema looked at the bus as it glided away. A passenger happened to catch her eye. They held each other's gaze as the bus passed. Prema's hand on the bag of aquamarine marbles, she saw the man on the bus and—through his eyes—saw herself in the Saturn, and thought: look. She had become one of those Americans she used to look at from the buses, those Americans whose lives she had wanted for herself.

Little Nepal

~

When, three years ago, her airplane had touched down at LAX, Prema had thought: I have reached America. It had not felt like America, though. The airport walls were ripped out for construction, the ceilings were exposed and the floors were covered with dust. The immigration line was disorderly. It took hours to get to the front. When her turn came, the official directed her to another line. The official there examined her forms, stamped her passport and fingerprinted her, saying, 'Welcome to America.' He was already looking past her to the next person in line.

Prema's suitcase arrived battered. At customs she had nothing to declare. Outside, she looked around at the waiting crowd, and saw a man carrying a sign: MISS PREMA.

The middleman's nephew immediately recognized her as a compatriot: 'Swaagat chha Americamaa,' he said. Pushing her luggage cart, he led her to a vast lot where his car was parked. They loaded the car, then drove out into a landscape abandoned to highways.

In the sudden sunlight, Prema blinked. There were road signs pointing straight, left, right. Date palms rose abruptly from the horizon. The middleman's nephew kept trying to engage her in conversation; but she was absorbed by the view ahead. There were no skyscrapers anywhere in sight. What exactly were the billboards advertising? They turned into a stretch of neighbourhoods that looked uninhabited, though there were stores, markets and lots full of cars. No parking. Tow-away zone. Left lane exit only. It was a crystal-clear morning sparkling with a clean blue light. Prema had expected it to be colder in America. The middleman's nephew told her it had rained the day before. Only later did she discover it rained in the wintertime here.

He drove her to a neighbourhood that he called Little Nepal. He had arranged for her to rent a room in the house of a compatriot family there. By the time they reached the sleepy, elm-lined neighbourhood of low, cream-coloured houses, Prema was overcome by jet lag. She met her host family—a portly husband and wife with two teenaged sons. They were lottery winners from the previous year. Without further formalities, the wife, Neeru, fed Prema daal-bhat and sent her to bed in a room set aside for her.

She never saw the middleman's nephew again. When she awoke the next day, the husband, Sushil, told her that his wife had gone to work. Neeru worked at an Indian restaurant where the middleman's nephew had also found a job for Prema. 'That's the best kind of work you can find when you first come to this country, Bahini,' Sushil explained to her delicately, as though to allay her disappointment. 'I myself deliver pizza for a fast-food chain. The work is easy; I get to sit at home all day. I have to work only when a call comes. I used to manage a paper mill back home. But here—' He shrugged good-naturedly.

Sushil and Neeru were in their forties, and half-modern, half-traditional: though Neeru worked full-time, she had to do all the cooking. Sushil cleaned the house and did the shopping, though; and he took their sons to school in the mornings.

Sushil was agreeable, but Neeru could be joyless. Despite her portly build, she had a drawn, pinched face made severe by big black eyeglasses. She wore baggy kurtha-surals, like any middle-class woman back home. She was extremely fond of dispensing advice. 'Bahini, you can't do anything in this country if you don't have a driver's licence,' Neeru told Prema on one of her early jet-lagged days. 'Your Sushil-bhinaju got his licence as soon as we got here. I'm going to take the written test soon so that I can get a permit. You can take the test in Hindi in the state of California.' She had a short, barking laugh. 'Imagine coming all the way to America to take a test in Hindi!'

Her husband smiled ruefully.

At the end of two weeks, Prema started to work at the restaurant alongside Neeru, in a nearby shopping complex. Walking there the first day along a wide boulevard, Neeru said, 'Back home, I thought this country would be—different. It's a nice country if you have money. If not— Now you tell me, Bahini, isn't this like any restaurant back home?'

The Shalimar, with a pig-pink facade and a string of outdoor lights by the front door. It—the entire shopping complex—looked defeated by weather: the sun, the wind, the dust. The owner, an aged Punjabi man, reigned over the cash till by the door, while his wife, Urmila-didi, oversaw the rest of the dark, oil-stained interior. The middleman's nephew had already got Prema hired as a kitchen hand; there was no interview. 'You're the new Nepali, hanh?' Urmila-didi said to her on the first day, by way of greeting. 'Bas, okay. Chalo. Let's get to work.'

In the kitchen, Prema met the cook, a compatriot named

Dhiraj. Ganga, the other kitchen hand, and the other waiters—Narayan and Shyam—were also from back home. 'Let's go, let's go,' Urmila-didi called out from the front room. Ganga and she set to vacuuming.

'Take this out. Clean that up. Close the door. Talk softly.' Urmila-didi was expert at issuing orders. She did not try to befriend the staff, though at one point in Prema's early weeks she said to her, thoughtfully, 'It's not like back home is it, Prema-behen? It's completely different here.'

Yet Neeru was right. This was like any restaurant back home. The occasional white person, and sometimes a Chinese or Filipino person, did come from offices nearby, but most of the customers were Indian: groups of men, or groups of women, or whole families gathering around the all-you-can-eat lunch buffets. There were no set breaks for the staff. When the lunchtime crowd thinned they took turns eating in a corridor that led out back to the trash bins. At five they started up again for the evening shift.

At the end of the night shift, Sushil would come to fetch Neeru and Prema, for it was unsafe to walk the streets after dark. Prema found their safety worries a bit strange. She found many things about America a bit strange. After dinner, in her room, she would stand by the window looking out through her binoculars at the tungsten-and-halogen sky.

Over the next few months, Sushil and Neeru took complete charge of Prema. Walking to the Shalimar in the morning, Neeru would tell her what she thought Prema needed to know to survive in this land: EZ Foods was expensive; the Lucky Money Mart—with dimly lit aisles of canned foods, frozen foods, bottled drinks and tired produce—was cheaper. 'Cold cut sandwiches are the easiest meals.' 'Everything is so expensive in this country. Never buy clothes at full price, Bahini. Always wait for a sale.' 'Always say thank you to foreigners.' When Neeru said 'foreigners', she meant Americans. Neeru taught her where to buy phone cards, where to check email, how to take the bus to the Department of Motor Vehicles and get a State of California identity card. She explained social security to Prema, and health care and unemployment benefits. She gave her the names of lawyers and social workers to turn to in case of crisis. On her advice, Prema opened an account at a Citibank branch in the neighbourhood. Against her advice, she applied for a credit card, but—having no credit history—was denied it. 'In six months you can have a card with a fifty-thousand dollar limit,' Neeru later scolded her, 'but you have to take the right steps. You can't just do anything you want to, Bahini, it's not like back home. You have to figure out the system first.' Neeru approached America like a grim puzzle that she was bent on solving. 'If you want to succeed here you have to work hard,' she would say. 'That's the one thing we Nepalis need to learn from the Indians: don't be ashamed to work hard.'

There was little more to Little Nepal than twenty-odd families living in cream-coloured houses, all belonging to the same landlord, a Marathi man who was said to have ties to the Mumbai underworld. Prema paid Neeru and Sushil a rent of 200 dollars for her room and an additional 100 for food and utilities. Neeru and Sushil often went to visit other compatriots, or had them over to their house. In the beginning Prema joined in, like a family member. Her compatriots formed a companionable huddle. Sushil would joke about pizza delivery, Neeru would quip about taking a driving test in Hindi, and the others, too, would share the absurdities of their lives here. Prema enjoyed their company, but sometimes, among them, she felt stuck on the outside of America. Her compatriots spoke in the Nepali language among themselves; and their talk invariably turned homeward: the Maoist rebels, the king and the army, the faltering movement for peace. They talked of Americans—'foreigners'—with some perplexity. 'Every time a black man comes into the shop, I'm worried he'll rob us,' one man said. 'Don't be friendly with Mexicans,' one woman told Prema every time they met: 'If they talk to you, just say no habla Español.' Another woman told her, 'Never trust the Chinese. Or the Koreans. And always watch out for Indians.' As though in all of America, only they and the white people were pure.

Prema did not feel that she had actually reached America. At the Shalimar, she did kitchen duty for four months. The staff were furtive about their private lives. Prema found out from Neeru that Ganga and Shyam were illegal; 'undocumented workers', she called them. Narayan had arrived years ago, on a student visa, now expired. The cook, Dhiraj, was looking for better options. After a few months Narayan went to live with a cousin in the state of Nebraska. A Punjabi woman named Reena came to work in his place. Then Shyam stopped coming. Neeru told Prema that he had gone to the state of Texas. He was replaced by a compatriot who went by the name BR. And then Ganga, too, left for the state of Florida, where he had people from his birth village.

Prema stayed on because she had nowhere to go. For six months, the middleman's nephew took a cut of her salary: she had to mail him a cheque. Nevertheless, because she had so few expenses, she built up modest savings. When the Punjabi woman, Reena, quit, Urmila-didi hired a new kitchen hand, Ram Bahadur, a twenty-year-old from back home. After that Prema began serving. The tips earned her a little extra.

As the months passed, Prema began to want to see what lay beyond Little Nepal. America was, so far, a land of little white houses, of lives bound in concrete, where the air smelled faintly of tar. It was very plain, and even ugly. There was a layered buzzing in the air, a constant drone that infiltrated even the most profound silence. On the boulevard to the shopping complex there were wax myrtle, cottonwood and laurel trees—native or imported? Prema could not tell. In the parking lot in front of the Shalimar, endless rows of cars: Toyota Sienna, Infiniti FX35, Saturn LS2. The breezes blew sometimes from the east, and sometimes from the west. Only gradually did she come to understand the weather systems they rode. Some days it rained as in the monsoon. Some days the light was iridescent, and the air glistened. Winter ended without the days getting too cold.

She couldn't keep track of how many things surprised her. This was—wasn't it?—a country at war. You would never be able to tell from the way people went about their days, unaffected. The newspapers sometimes carried stories of Iraq and Afghanistan; but on television most of what she saw were dramas, home-decorating shows, talk shows, advertisements for colon cleansing, action films, poker—'The best hand you can get, the wheel, the bicycle. Will he call it?'—and advertisements: full-coverage insurance, shoe week, everything must go, a forty-dollar value for nineteen ninety-nine and a sixty-dollar value for absolutely free.

She found it just as disorienting to walk the neighbourhood.

In a metropolis of millions, there were only ever a few people walking on the pavements. Where was everyone? She had not known there were so many Latino, Asian and African American people in America. When someone spoke to her, she was invariably taken for Mexican: '¿Qué hora es?' '¿A hacia dónde va la camioneta?' One day two young men in baggy jeans came up to her at an intersection. One said something in Spanish.

'No habla Español,' she replied, remembering her compatriot's advice.

'¿Por qué no?' he demanded.

She tried again: 'No habla Español.'

He snorted. 'Yo, chica, it's cool. We're all one, you must not deny, we must not be 'shamed of our heritage—'

Till his friend hissed, 'No es Latina, man.'

The man paused. '¿Ella no?'

'Ella es India,' the friend said. To Prema he said: 'You from India, ain't you?'

'I am from Nepal,' Prema said.

'Na what?'

'Near India.'

'Shit, I coulda sworn. You look Mexican,' the first man exclaimed.

'Thank you,' Prema said.

When Prema got home, she told Neeru about this exchange, only to have Neeru cry in alarm: 'Never talk to Mexican men, Bahini, they want only one thing from a pretty girl like you!'

'I didn't talk,' Prema said. 'I told them, no habla Español.'

But Neeru kept crying: 'Never, never talk to Mexican men. It is not safe! Next time, just say: no soy Mexican. No, no! Say: *no soy Mexicana. That's* what you have to say!'

To Reach America

~

'So when was the last time you called home?' Luis asked on their next date, at a restaurant in Chinatown so clattery they had to shout to hear themselves talk.

'A long time,' Prema shouted back.

'If you ever want to use my cell, really—' He said, 'Any time you want to call and say hey guys, I'm fine, how are things with you?'

She smiled. 'We do not say *hi.* Or *you guys.*'

'You know what I mean.'

'It is all right,' she said.

She did not lie to Luis about anything. Just—some topics never came up. He did not think to ask about them; and, it did not occur to her to volunteer.

She had deliberately cut off contact with home. Early on in Little Nepal, she had bought a phone card and telephoned her birth village. After the operator had fetched her father, she had told him she had found work. 'Chhori, you're on your way, then,' he had said in his soft, gravelly voice. She had agreed: 'Yes, Ba.' She did not offer to send him money: what little she earned at the Shalimar she needed for herself. Nor did he ask her to send any. Still, when she hung up, she felt she had abandoned him, and her sister, to their broken fates. The war. She didn't know what to do with this feeling. She never called home again.

She stopped looking up the news of Nepal on the Internet, and let her email account expire. Instead, she scoured the newspapers for information about America: unemployment was up, the housing figures were down, the president's popularity was dipping. A diner in Pasadena had closed after thirty years of operation, and a man had been found dead at the bottom of the San Pedro cliff. On the back page: *Breakfast benefit for Veterans. Worship: 11 a.m. and 6 p.m. Do you have difficulty falling asleep? Are you losing your hair? Walk for peace. Shots for tots and teens. Adult cabaret, totally nude dancers.*

To reach America, she began to take the buses—the No. 130 or the No. 127 or the No. 128 or the No. 20—their scratched and tinted windows like screens into lives she couldn't have. Americans driving one person to a car. She wanted their lives for herself. She would catch the bus to Lomita, Burbank, Yorba Linda—anywhere—mesmerized by the way the highways merged and divided, divided and merged. One day she reached the skyscrapers downtown. The lamp posts flew by as the bus whizzed below the underpasses. The wealthier the neighbourhood the greener it was in this land. In the poor areas, there was one decrepit building, another decrepit building, and another: for miles. It reminded her of the town at the base of the hills. One rutted street, another rutted street, another. Once, she saw a shop with a giant yellow doughnut on the roof. A doughnut shop. On the roads downtown, she sat resigned to not getting anywhere soon. On the freeways, though, the buses were alight at the speed of traffic. Now and again she glimpsed the ocean: a gleaming strip of silver in the distance.

Her directions changed constantly in the open avenues and depopulated streets of the metropolis. 'You're on your way,' her father had said on the telephone. He had thought she was progressing. But she felt lucky just to be surviving. She would get off at a stop—Wilshire, La Brea, Bellflower—and take connections, committing the landscape to memory. 91 East. 405 North. Alameda. Rosecrans. The low boxy buildings. The Imperial Highway. The concrete-block divisions. The street lamps in a row. Traffic lights in a snarl of wires. The shopping complexes and the parking lots. Avocaten. Hair and Nails. El Pueblo Hardware. Check Cashing. Karey's Beauty Supply.

Prema left Little Nepal as abruptly as she had left Nepal. One summer's day a year after her arrival, she saw some greenery from the bus. She got off at the next stop, before a clutter of groaning old buildings—Upper Mind Church Daily Donut Smoothie JESUS S VES Cappuccino—and made her way back to the greenery. MacArthur Park.

It was crowded in the park; there was a street fair on. Everyone was speaking Spanish, and she assumed they were Mexican till she saw a sign: Republic de el Salvador en la America Central. Enjoying the crowded feel, Prema pressed past the stalls hawking breads, meats, bottled drinks, and handmade dolls, glass beads, tours to Costa Rica. At one stall people were shooting at stuffed animals with toy guns. There were clothes for sale at another stall, and on a whim she bought a low-cut indigo dress. At another stall she bought a field guide to Southern California. Somewhere, a band was playing Spanish pop songs. A group of women walked by wearing CALIFORNIA PARA JESUCRISTO T-shirts. A man at a legal-aid booth handed her a brochure: El Rescate.

There was not much to the park: a grassy slope landscaped with palm trees and an artificial pond. There was a fountain in the pond. People were riding paddle boats around it. Prema watched them awhile.

On the way back to the bus stop, she passed a building with high Greek columns. Its front doors were open. Some people were walking in. On a whim she followed them in.

And found herself in a fluorescent-lit corridor lined, on both sides, with posters for the LA Metropolitan Alliance; Janitors for Justice; the American Federation of State, County and Municipal Employees. Beyond a door, a meeting of some kind was in progress. Prema stayed in the corridor, looking at the posters. The LA Living Wages Coalition. The Korean Immigrant Workers Advocates. Posters for unions for homecare workers, garment workers, food-service workers. The Pilipino Workers Center. Above another door were two hand-painted slogans: Boycott Coors. WAL-MART NO. Prema felt a pang of regret. Had she stayed in touch with Rajan, she could have emailed him: there are labour unions in America, did you know? And they could have communicated…

At the far end of the corridor she reached a notice board tacked with announcements: advertisements for tutoring, furniture, phone sex, dog walking, carpools, babysitting. Apartments for lease: *2 Bdr Victorian in Los Feliz No Smokers Call Stan. Lrg brt 1 bdrm, D/F, FP, Patio. 2 + 1, upper, stove, blinds, carpets. Tile fer, refig, 1 cr sec prkg.* One notice said: *Shared house, Available Immediately. 400/month! Women only!*

She tore off the notices, and on the bus back to Little Nepal reread them, one by one. She had worked at the Shalimar for a year. She had savings of almost two thousand dollars. She wanted to reach America.

To reach America, she telephoned about tutoring, but they were looking for math instructors. She telephoned about dog walking, but the pay was too low. She telephoned about babysitting, but it was too few hours. She did not call Stan about the two-bedroom in Los Feliz. Nor did she call about the other one-bedroom. She did call the number for the shared house, women only—and, a few days later, she took the bus past the skyscrapers downtown to a dry, grassy hill by a dishevelled boulevard.

All the houses on the hill were rickety. Prema went up to a toothpaste-green house with iron grills at the windows. After she rang the bell she heard the sound of three latches opening.

A black—African American—woman answered the door. 'Heya. You Prima? I'm Meg. Come on in. That's such a pretty name, Prima. Is it Italian?'

'Nepali.'

'Napoli?'

'Near India.'

'I love chicken vindaloo!' Meg showed Prema to the common room. 'There's a great Indian restaurant just across from the Keck, that's where I go, but every time I end up ordering the same thing because I know I'll love it—are you like that? Their vindaloo is to die for! But I also love the breads. Do you know how to make naan, Prima? Guess you'd need a special oven for that, huh. Anyways. How long ago did you come here, Prima?'

Before Prema could answer, Meg went on, 'Aw, don't mind me, I shouldn't ask, I don't really care if you're not— I mean, everyone except the Native Americans are immigrants in this country.' She smiled. 'My mom just found out she's got Ashanti blood. Anyways. The woman who shared the house moved out: didn't even care about forfeiting her deposit. No skin off my back. I manage the house for Henry Little—that's the landlord. He isn't picky, but me, I can't live with just anyone. There's been a lot of calls, someone else is coming by to see it later. But if you can pay the deposit I'll keep the place for you.'

'I can write a cheque,' Prema said.

'That would work.'

Prema wrote out the cheque.

Meg startled her by lunging at her with a bear-like hug. 'Welcome, housemate!' Prema lay limp in her embrace till she let go.

Meg walked her out to the front door. 'Well, I better get back to my studies. I'm studying nursing, figure I'll be able to help people, save the world and all. There are so many nurses from India here. Anyways. You coming next weekend, Prima? I'll make you a set of keys.'

Prema left the house to the sound of three latches closing.

Neeru got very upset when Prema said she was leaving. Neeru reddened, took off her eyeglasses, wiped them on her kurtha, and put them back on, glaring. 'How will you get by in this land, Bahini,' she sputtered, 'when you don't even know how to drive?'

Sushil intervened. 'Eh, our Bahini isn't a child.'

'It's dangerous out there!' Neeru cried. 'Who'll look out for her?'

'Eh, let her try,' Sushil said gently, as though the decision were his wife's to make.

But Neeru only grew angrier. 'It won't be like here! She's being foolish! We have to stick together. How— She— We've done everything for her! She doesn't know the first thing about this land!'

'She'll manage, don't worry, she'll manage,' Sushil clucked.

'Let her go, then, go. Go! Let's see how far she gets!' Neeru cried vindictively.

As though Prema were abandoning them. It made her feel—guilty. And also angry. What claim did Neeru and Sushil have on her?

She quit the Shalimar, and the following Saturday she moved, ordering a taxi even though Sushil had offered to drive her. She did not want him and Neeru to know where she was going. She wanted to leave, just—go. Get as far away as she could from the past.

Neeru watched sourly as she loaded her suitcase into the taxi's boot. Then she bade Prema a stern farewell. 'What you don't know is that foreigners aren't like us, Bahini. A cold blood flows through their veins. Watch out for your safety, don't let anyone take advantage, and remember your own people.' Suddenly, tears welled up in her eyes. 'If you ever need us, you don't even have to call,' she said. 'You know where we are. Just come.'

Then, unexpectedly, she hugged Prema in the American way, but awkwardly. Their arms got in the way, blocking.

Sushil and she exchanged polite namastes. 'Call us when you get there,' he said.

'I will,' Prema lied.

Her heart started pounding as the taxi took off, as Little Nepal receded, block after block. The taxi driver took the underpass into downtown, past the skyscrapers, to the dishevelled boulevard. Finally, she thought as she got off on the dry, grassy hill with rickety houses. Thinking: I have reached America at last.

The Hunger, the Wanting

~

Neeru was right. It was not easy to survive in America. From the next day on, Prema began to hunt the neighbourhood for 'Employment' and 'Opening' signs. A man at a Cream Shoppe asked, '¿Habla Español?' and turned away rolling his eyes when she replied, 'No soy Mexicana.' There was a vacancy sign on the window of a 7-11, but a man inside said the position had been filled. She passed an entire row of boarded-up shops and restaurants. She passed a Title Company, wondering what they did, and the Tokyo Massage, and a signboard: *This Sign for Lease: (818) 540-3491.* The boulevard was littered with paper, tin cans, rags and clothes, plastic bags that fluttered in the wind. It was as shabby as any Third World country here.

Several days in, a pasty, red-haired man at Wally's Beer and Wine said he would pay her twenty-five dollars if she cleaned up his storeroom. Remembering Neeru's advice—don't be ashamed to work hard—Prema spent the afternoon mopping the floor as a dormouse scurried from aisle to aisle, fleeing for its life.

The red-haired man was kindly. At the end of the day, on top of her payment, he gave her a sandwich and a Snapple. 'You looking for work, Miss? There's a store there.' He pointed across the way. 'The old lady lost a worker a few days ago. She doesn't like Mexicans, but you can give it a try.'

Korean Supplies: Hangul lettering in red and English lettering in blue. Inside, when Prema asked if there was a vacancy, the proprietor, an elderly Korean woman, looked at her sharply. 'Where you from?' she demanded.

Prema hesitated, then said, 'I am from India.'

'You work in shop before?'

She said no, but she had worked in a restaurant.

'You work hard? You no lazy?'

She said she worked hard and was not lazy.

The proprietor said, 'Okay we try for two weeks. If no like, no job! When you start? Tomorrow? Tomorrow. You come seven, sharp. Sharp!'

So began a lonely year of stocking the shelves with tinned food, bottled drinks, packaged meats, all labelled in Hangul. Prema came to recognize products by their graphics. Early on, the proprietor, Mrs Han Sung, hovered near her; but she relaxed as Prema proved trustworthy. Mrs Han Sung was a devout Christian. At the cash register she read books about souls awaiting God's love, revelations that would heal hearts in need of saving. She sometimes asked Prema if she wanted to borrow them. Out of politeness Prema would say yes. 'You like?' Mrs Han Sung would ask enthusiastically when she returned the books. 'I liked,' Prema would lie. And Mrs Han Sung would loan her another one.

Prema never had occasion to speak in Nepali any more. She hardly had occasion to speak at all. Most of the shop's customers spoke Korean. Mrs Han Sung dealt with their queries. Twice a week, early in the morning, two Korean men, both called Kim, made deliveries in a white van. Neither spoke much English, but both were friendly, giving Prema small gifts—fermented pickles, rice cakes, dried fish. When they finished their deliveries she would watch them leave, imagining vans like theirs making deliveries to shops all over this strange land.

Prema's pay at Korean Supplies was minimum wage, what she had made at the Shalimar after tips. Her rent was higher, though. Back in the hill bazaar, Prema had had two hundred thousand rupees in her bank account—a small fortune by Nepali measure. In coming to America she had become poor. The savings she had built up at the Shalimar were dwindling. On payday Prema would count each dollar carefully: *this note is legal tender for all debts, public and private.* She felt desperate, and—was this what poverty did?—she felt hungry, wanting.

Korean Supplies closed at six. The dishevelled boulevard looked dangerous at night. At home Prema would eat a sandwich—cold cuts of ham, pastrami, roast beef—as rats scurried in the kitchen corners. After dinner, alone in her room, she would scan the back pages of the local newspapers—*Have credit cards with high limits, low balances? Women 18–32 earn $5000 donating eggs to infertile couples. Avoid bankruptcy: call now for FREE ten minute consultation. Earn $5,000 to $10,000/ month*—wondering whether to believe these offers.

She missed Sushil and Neeru, and the company of her compatriots in Little Nepal. But she was determined to keep going farther. On her days off she would go downtown among the skyscrapers, getting off the bus at the concert hall. She would circle its glinting, curved exterior. Then she would walk to the overpass with the cars on the freeway underfoot. She would look up at the skyscrapers: outcroppings of rocks igneous, sedimentary, metamorphic. She would walk the stepped streets of downtown, the pedestrian walkways, the abrupt tunnels and landscaped footpaths. The high financial streets would all be empty, the plaza benches abandoned. She would sit there getting her fill of glass and granite. What she had once thought all of America would be like.

Then she would walk a few blocks to the ramshackle low streets, where the shops were always open, hawking shoes, bags, belts, T-shirts, CDs. Here, everyone looked—Mexican? Latino. She blended right in. The signs on the shops announced: Employment Bilingual. Bridal shop windows with sequin-encrusted gowns and matching shoes, bags, tiaras. SE SOLICITA MODISTA CON EXPERIENCIA. Money transfer. ¡SE HABLA ESPAÑOL! At a street-side stall Prema would have a soft drink and a savoury pastry called an empanada. Then, past armies of homeless men in an open square, she would catch the bus back to the dishevelled boulevard. Wondering—*This* is America? It was neither proper nor solid. How could anyone from the ramshackle streets move up to the streets of glass and granite? Alone in her room, she would look over the newspapers, scanning the classified pages. *Amateur models wanted. $1050/ week mailing brochures from home. $360,000/year opportunity. $$ FREE $$ CASH $$ NEVER REPAY!* Or she would take out her binoculars and look past the iron grills at the window, at the neighbours. Feeling something. Not homesick, but something like it. She missed something. Not her compatriots. Her compatriots, she could return to in Little Nepal. She could even go back to Nepal if it came to that. That was not what she missed. What, then?

Whatever it was, she tried to get it through Andy.

Andy Campbell: a foreigner, Neeru and Sushil would have called him. White, with blond hair and brown eyes, and deep, sunken creases through his cheeks when he smiled. He moved to the street after buying a house, a rickety adobe across the way. Prema noticed him when he began to remodel it, gutting the interior and scraping the paint off the exterior, and strewing the site with planks, pipes, ladders and construction tools.

He would smile at her, creasing his cheeks, every time she passed. She would smile back. One day, when she was walking by with heavy grocery bags, he crossed over to help carry them. At her front door he held out a hand: 'Heya, I'm Andy. Andy Campbell.'

'I am Prema.'

'Drop by my place sometime, Pray-muh.'

She didn't drop by. But she did stand at the window a few times, looking at him. He had a sportsman's build: loose-limbed and agile, like an elegant animal, a gazelle.

The next few times they passed each other, Andy would call out: 'Heya, Pray-muh.' And she would call back: 'Hello Andy.' And soon they had said 'Heya Pray-muh,' and 'Hello Andy,' so often it felt as though they knew each other.

'One moment, Pray-muh,' Andy called out one day, skipping off a stepladder. He came up to her on the pavement. 'You like live music, Pray-muh? There's this band, Nuclear Energy, they have an open house tonight at this bar right down the street. Want to check it out?'

To allay her hunger, her wanting, she said all right.

'Sweet.' His cheeks creased. 'How's seven?'

She nodded.

'See ya there, Pray-muh.'

'Bye.'

That evening she put on the indigo dress she had bought at the Salvadorian street fair. This was the first time she was wearing it, the first time she saw that it made her look like a Bollywood heroine.

Susan swept into the house just as she was about to leave. 'Oh, honey, that's hot!'

'I have a date,' Prema announced: 'The man who is making the house.'

'Mr Home Builder, next door? Oh, he's all right.' Susan winked. 'I went out with him last week, he's a stud. You know what you'll need, though?' She rummaged through her handbag and brought out a plastic pack. A condom. 'Keep this handy,' she said. 'I mean it! A girl's gotta watch out for herself!' Then she hugged Prema. 'Oh, honey, knock 'em dead!'

Thrown off balance by this, Prema walked to the bar on the dishevelled boulevard. Though the bar was dingy on the outside, it was lively inside. Andy was standing at a counter, dressed in jeans and a tight, shiny T-shirt. He had spiked his hair up with gel.

He smiled. 'Beer, Pray-muh?'

She nodded.

He ordered two Heinekens.

Andy had a curious way of talking. He would ask a question, then talk about himself for a while, then ask another question, always inserting her name in, as though to remind himself who he was talking to: 'So Pray-muh,' he started. 'You like music?'

'Yes.'

'Nuclear Energy's amazing. I love these guys, saw them last year—right here! You like garage-house rock, Pray-muh?'

'I do not know it.'

'What kinda music you like, Pray-muh?'

'I like'—she searched for a name—'Clint Black.'

'A country-western kinda gal, are ya? These guys—you'll see—they're fantastic. So, Pray-muh, what do you do for work?'

He was in the business of buying and renovating houses. 'It's a lot of speculation, Pray-muh, which neighbourhood's heading up, which is heading down. This boom can't last forever, but I've been doing this awhile, I've got a sense of the market. You have to know when to flip. I could advise you if you want. You a renter or a buyer, Pray-muh? If you're thinking of buying around here, the prices are sure to rise—there's a lot of history here, and people are willing to shell out big bucks for that. So where in Mexico you from, Pray-muh?'

Was there any point in mentioning Nepal? Prema said, 'I am from India.'

'Oh, I thought—' He said, 'I mean, I like Mexican girls. My last real girlfriend was Puerto Rican. She was crazy—not bad, cuckoo crazy, but good crazy, all into Puerto Rican independence. So. India.' He said, 'What's India like, Pray-muh?'

'It is nice.'

'That's in Asia, isn't it? Know what? I never dated an Asian woman.'

Prema had never thought of herself as an Asian woman.

From a stage in a corner of the bar, a band started up. 'Oh, here they come.' Andy ordered two more Heinekens, and then they sat back and listened. The bar was crowded by then, and as the music blasted so did everyone's voices. When Andy and she talked—'More beer, Pray-muh?' 'No thank you, Andy!'—they had to shout.

Afterwards she went with him to his house, Susan's words—knock 'em dead—ringing inside her. Was that an expression about sex? Should she—? Casual sex. From what she had seen by observing Susan, the chances that you would take to a near-stranger were slim, but you had sex with him anyway, because otherwise you would never know.

'I'm going to start plastering soon,' Andy said, walking her through the demolished interior to an independent unit at the back, where he lived. 'The plumbing's fixed and I'll be finished with the wiring in a few days. I'm going to see if I can rent it out next month, Pray-muh.'

They stood in his small kitchen as he drank another Heineken. Through Andy's shiny, tight T-shirt Prema could see his impressive musculature. When he moved closer she did not move away. When he kissed her she kissed him back. But when he held her she could not help thinking of Rajan.

'You're real pretty, Pray-muh,' Andy whispered.

She did not know what else to say: 'You are handsome, Andy.'

He led her to his bedroom and sat her on his bed. When, after telling her again how pretty she was, he began to run his hands over her, she did not resist. He undid her dress. 'You're real pretty, Pray-muh.'

'You are handsome, Andy.'

Eventually they were both naked. Would he produce a condom? Prema wondered: should she bring out the one Susan had given her? Despite all that musculature Andy turned into a soft mass of flesh when horizontal. She lay below him, squashed and uncertain. From the way he was squirming she thought this was foreplay, till she realized he was about to penetrate.

'Um. Andy. Birth control?' she blurted out.

He became still. 'What's that you said, Pray-muh?'

'Do you have a condom, Andy?'

'Aw, I hate those things,' he said. 'Don't worry, Pray-muh, I'll be careful.'

He began to squirm again.

'What about AIDS?' she said.

'You got AIDS?' he said.

'It is not safe.'

'Aw, I hate condoms!'

'I brought one,' she said.

He rolled off with a sigh. She took out the condom. He put it on. Then they had sex till he came.

'Was it all right?' he asked, afterwards. 'Was it all right, Pray-muh?'

'Yes,' she said. And it had been. He hadn't made her do anything she hadn't wanted to. She had had sex. American sex. Casual sex, even.

She got out of bed.

'Aw, you can stay the night, Pray-muh, you don't have to go.'

'No, I have to go.'

She dressed hurriedly. Andy also put on his clothes, and walked her across the street in the dark. At the front door he kissed her as though they were boyfriend and girlfriend.

'That was real special, Pray-muh. See you 'round?'

'Bye.'

Inside, she bolted the three latches and hugged herself tightly.

Every now and then, she passed Andy on the street, and though they exchanged a few lingering greetings, they did not go out again. And soon he was as indistinct in her mind as the blur she saw from the bus on the freeway, moving at speed.

Prema's hunger, her wanting, remained, as did her desire for what, she did not know. In the evenings she kept scanning the back pages—desperate—till one day Meg said, entirely in passing, 'I should just give up nursing and take up elderly care. The pay is decent—and I wouldn't have to go through nursing school.'

After that, Prema began to scan the back pages more purposefully: *Do you want to give the family freedom from the stress of caring for a loved one? Serve the elderly with non-medical companionship and help in their homes.*

The first few calls she placed she hesitated, and the person on the other end grew impatient: 'You're calling about the opening?' 'Speak up, I can't hear you.' In time she learned to say, 'I am telephoning about the notice. I would like to apply for the job.'

Natalie eventually hired her as Esther's homecare attendant.

An American Relationship

~

'I love you.' 'I love you.' Each time Luis and she said this, it sounded more resonant, true. How easily they slipped into a relationship. That this was a relationship, or what the Americans called a relationship, Prema was certain. She had learned as much from Meg and Susan. Susan used to call what she did with men *dating.* When she was not around, though, Meg called it *sleeping around*, and said Susan would never have a relationship because she slept around. Meg's relationship with her boyfriend Luke was—as she often told Prema—a *committed* relationship, which, Prema gathered, was what one had after being in a relationship awhile. From this Prema deduced that Luis and she were no longer dating; they were in a relationship, and they seemed to be heading inexorably towards commitment.

'God, I love you.'

This, despite the gaps—small and large—in their worlds. Some gaps were minor, such as the fact of Luis's spiritual life. He meditated every morning, and called this his practice. He would sit cross-legged on a cushion on the floor, his eyes closed and his expression slack. He would remain motionless for twenty minutes, sometimes with a half-smile creeping over his lips. Prema just found this queer.

Other gaps arose from the English language: misunderstood words or phrases. One time, when Luis described himself as a regular Joe, and Prema said, 'I do not think you are like an army man.' 'What?' he said. 'Is regular Joe not an army man?' He said, 'No, no, you're thinking of GI Joe. A regular Joe's someone kind of—like me. You know, normal.'

Other times, he would tell her things she already knew: 'Soccer is what you would call football.' Or he would over-explain things, repeating jokes or substituting less local terms in his expressions, describing his supervisor at Meadowvale, a woman called Janet Daly, as an idiot instead of a jerk, though Prema knew by now what 'jerk' meant. Once, he said, 'Sometimes people get very, very angry when they drive,' instead of using the term 'road rage', which she had read of in *Los Angeles Times* online during her last weeks in the capital, back in Nepal. 'Yes,' Prema said, 'I understand.' Then Luis would assume she understood other words; and she would be left having to ask: 'What does hunky-dory mean?' 'What is doo-wop?' Then again he would start to over-explain things: 'There's this fault line called the San Andreas…' 'Yes,' Prema said: 'The Pacific plate is pushing up against the North American continent, I know.'

Such confusion was to be expected; but it did make Prema wonder what they did and did not know about the other.

Prema asked Luis, one day, about his father. 'His name was Carlos Reyes-Garcia, originally. But he went by Carl Reyes,' he said. 'Was an engineer at the Department of Public Works. What about your family?' he asked. 'I don't even know your sister's name. You know, you always just call her "my sister". Tell me about her—what's she do? And what about your parents?'

Prema did not tell Luis that Bijaya was a Maoist. How could she possibly explain such a thing to an American? Instead, she told him that in Nepal it was impolite to call people by name alone. 'Bahini,' she said, 'means younger sister. My sister's name is Bijaya, but I call her Bahini.' She added, 'My mother's name was Rewati. My father is Gokul.'

The names transformed to Bee-jay, Ray-wetty and Go-call on Luis's tongue.

Another evening, Luis asked, 'What's an engine-o?'

'An engine-o?'

'You said you used to work for an engine-o.'

'An NGO. You know non-government organization?'

'Oh. Is that like a 501-c?'

'A what?'

Development, to him, meant fundraising. To her it encapsulated the entire task of nation-building. It was like that. There was much they did not quite grasp. And— It was not late in their lives, but neither was it so early. It did not seem possible to share their pasts completely. To try to do so would disrupt the amnesiac present.

Soon Prema got to know all Luis's friends. Americans. They were all so…exotic. Jim and Berry Landermann, whose daughter Gemma was July's friend, lived across the plaza, on 109th. Jim was a dental assistant and Berry a paralegal. Another friend of his, Rob Hess, was recently separated from his wife, and lacking for company. He was an internist. At Meadowvale, Luis introduced Prema to a few colleagues: a nurse, Dinita Martinez, whom he had once dated, and Wayne Chu, in the accounts department. Luis also told her about his closest friends, Steve

Adams and Camilla Arguelles, with whom he had lost touch after his ex-wife had remarried. Steve was a recording engineer at an easy listening station. Camilla taught athletics at a private girls' school. 'They were like family,' Luis said. 'It wasn't like they took sides, but somehow— They're close to Tina and this dork she married, Christopher, and I don't know. It still feels a bit weird.'

One Sunday, Luis invited Prema for lunch with him and his daughter July. 'She's the person who matters the most in my life,' he said. 'I want her to get to know you.'

And Prema realized this had turned into a committed relationship.

They agreed to meet at the Galleria, an indoor shopping complex of the kind the Americans called a mall. It fell on a major bus route. Prema entered through a store full of men's suits. Inside, the automatic doors slid open to a vestibule which rose, floor upon floor. Luis had told her to go to the top floor. There was an escalator past a lingerie shop, but only when Prema got to it did she see it was coming down, not going up. The up escalator was across a fountain, where two grown men were licking ice cream cones. Prema rode the escalator past shops selling women's clothing, handbags, shoes, bath products, books, sports gear, CDs, socks, hairpins, soaps, dishes, toys. The air smelled of talcum powder. On the top floor, children were riding a toy rocket. Prema stopped at a thicket of neon signs: Hot Dog on a Stick. Red Rock Chili Company. McDonald's. El Pollo Loco. Panda Express.

'Hey.' Luis put an arm around her.

July was with him. At seven she looked like a teenager: her hair was braided in the African style, and—Prema was surprised to see—her eyes were elongated, East Asian.

'Prema, meet July,' Luis said. 'July, this is Prema. My girlfriend.'

'Does that mean you sleep in the same bed?' July said.

Prema baulked.

But Luis was unfazed. 'Yeah,' he said. 'We also hold hands sometimes.'

'And kiss. Nora—that's my stepsister,' July explained for Prema's benefit, 'Nora has a boyfriend. Charlie Barker. She l-o-o-oves Charlie Barker. They kiss!'

'All right, who's hungry?' Luis turned to Prema. 'July's going to have a burger, as always. What will you have, Prema? There's Chinese stir-fry over there, which isn't bad, or beef burritos. Have you ever had chili? I think there's also Thai on the other end. They have some really good soups. Hot dogs? Or there's good old Mickey D.'

'Anything,' Prema said.

'There's also Indian at the far side. Or how about a Greek salad?'

'Anything.'

They all just got hamburgers, French fries and Cokes.

'You ever eat quarter-pounders, Prema?' Luis asked after they were seated.

'No.'

He turned to July. 'See? People from more evolved cultures don't eat junk food.'

'Well, Mom never lets me eat meat at home, so I've got to eat it when I'm with you, or I'll end up being a shortie, like her! 'Cause as we all know, Asians aren't the tallest people in the world.'

'Your mother is Asian?' Prema asked.

'Chinese-American.'

'Yeah, didn't I mention?' Luis said.

July turned back to her father. 'Dad, can we get some Ben & Jerry's after lunch?'

'No, never.'

She smiled triumphantly. 'That means yes! Is there Ben & Jerry's in Nepal, Prema?'

'There is another company. What is the name? Baskin-Robbins.'

'No kidding,' Luis said. 'Thirty-one flavours and all?'

After lunch, they took the escalators down, to an ice cream shop by the fountain. July tasted several flavours before choosing one. Luis and she went to the counter to pay. Prema waited by the door looking out at the mall, so strange. A few women were hunting through the shops with a determined expression. Distracted children were straggling behind their parents. Couples were ambling by, as in a park. Prema thought back to what Luis had said, early on, about life in America being about working and shopping and paying taxes and dying. It was not true that Luis's life was empty. Yet— She was not the only one who was adrift. Perhaps it is the same for people everywhere, Prema thought. Our lives are a catalogue of random occurrences that hew us into who we are, or who we think we are. We drift from circumstance to circumstance, pointing to the attributes that result from our adaptations and say: This is who I am. Luis had been searching for something, something elemental—meaning what? Universal? Not artificial. Authentic. Something like that. And he had found this—in her?

This thought stirred something in Prema, something tender, something protective. Love? A sweet, mute emotion.

A few weeks later, Luis suggested she move into his flat, and she readily said yes.

She was going to move in with her boyfriend!

She wanted to share the news with someone, anyone. A friend. Meg. But when she told Meg, Meg cried, 'Oh no! This means I'll have to find another tenant! I really didn't need this right now, Prima! The workload at school is unbelievable! And my brother just split up from his wife, I was planning to go and visit, now I'll have to cancel. Damn, Prima, this is really bad timing for me!'

It hurt her that Meg should give no thought to her happiness.

She never got to say a proper goodbye to Meg, as Meg was out on her last night in the house. Susan was home that night, brewing beer in the kitchen. She had turned on the television in the common room and was watching from the stove, where she was stirring a pot of barley water. When Prema went in, Susan pointed, with a spatula, at a plastic bag: 'Pass me the hops, honey?'

Prema passed the bag to her and watched as Susan sprinkled dry, green sheaves into the barley water.

'You want a beer, honey? I've got lots left from the old batch.'

'No, thank you.'

'It's a hundred per cent organic! And the yeast is really good for you.'

On the television screen, a man came riding a horse through a desert twilight. His face was chiselled and swarthy, and he was wearing what looked like a cowboy hat.

'Looks like this guy I'm dating,' Susan said. 'Wonderguy—he's from Uruguay! What are the men from India like, honey?'

'They are nice,' Prema said.

'Wonderguy's stellar!'

On the television screen the man got off his horse in front of a tent. In the next shot he was talking to a woman at a stove. Then he was tucking a child into bed, beneath heavy woollen blankets.

Mongolia.

A Mongolian family living in the kind of tent Rajan had told her about. A ger.

A voice-over on the television said the country was rebuilding itself from the ruins of communism.

The television show ended in a stream of credits. Susan started to pour the barley water into a holding tank. Prema returned to her room without saying goodbye to her. What was the point? Her time in this toothpaste-green house had been like a hallucination, here and gone. She wouldn't recognize either of her housemates if she were to pass them on the streets a few years later. Nothing about their acquaintance had any density.

The next morning Luis came to pick her up, and she left the dry, grassy hill. For a toy street in a plaza.

She spent the day unpacking. Her clothes fit easily into the closet and her books on a living-room shelf. She showed Luis her mother's ammonite. 'A fossil from when the himals were in the ocean.' She ran his fingers along the coiled exoskeleton. 'My mother believed it was the god Bishnu. That is what Hindus think.'

'Just blows your mind, doesn't it, stuff like that?'

She placed it on the bedside table, along with the bag of aquamarine marbles.

That night, Prema and Luis both felt celebratory. They started playing with each other in the kitchen, after he put a chicken to roast, and then they stumbled to the living room, tearing off each other's clothes, rolling off the sofa to the floor amid growls, shrieks, squeals. Luis's fingers on Prema's lips, his breath on her neck, her cries and pleas. He pressed her, naked, against the wall, and had her there; then they threw themselves into the bedroom. 'Make love to me everywhere,' Prema cried. 'I'll make love to you here. And here. And here,' Luis said, giving her the force of his coming.

Afterwards, they lay in bed laughing about having used up all the sex spots on their first night of living together. 'We'll have to find others,' he said. 'God, I love you, Prema. You know that? I really love you.' Prema said, 'I love you too.' 'Gimme a kiss,' he said. They kissed. And held each other, glistening, wet and radiant—till Luis bolted up, shouting, 'The chicken, the chicken! I forgot about the chicken!' and dashed naked to the kitchen, Prema trailing behind, also naked, doubled over and sputtering to catch her breath, laughing.

The God Within

~

With Luis Prema launched into a whole other—American—life, a proper and solid life at last. In their flat on their toy street, she would wake up, each morning, to a sky glimmering to candescence, to chrome. A door would slam somewhere, a car engine would fire on the street. In the bedroom, Luis's breath and hers. When the coffeemaker switched on with a faint clack in the kitchen, she would instinctively glance at the ammonite on her bedside table. Luis would sigh and turn over in bed, stretch an arm and leg across her.

Luis showered as she brewed tea for herself, she showered as he meditated. They had fruit and curd—yogurt—for breakfast. Luis drove her to and from work now. By 7.45 they would be in the Saturn listening to traffic reports. Road construction on the 110 northbound would have caused a back-up past Wilshire, a pickup with a flat would have skidded to a halt on the Santa Monica freeway. The tow truck would be on the way but commuters could expect delays. The sun would glint off the skyscrapers by the high-tension wires, near the traffic lights at the underpass. From there Luis would turn on to the wetlands, and beyond, past the Home Wart, to Esther's street. 'Love you,' he would say, pulling up to the curb. 'I love you,' Prema would say. They would kiss. And she would get out to the coast and the roar of airplanes at LAX.

In the evenings Luis would pick her up, and if they were not going out, they would stop by the plaza, and at Gabrielino Groceries they would walk from aisle to aisle, conjuring up recipes. 'Pasta?' 'We had that day before yesterday.' 'Stir-fry?' Over dinner they would go over their day. She would tell him about the things Esther had said: 'There is a temple—church?—called Hagia Sophia.' He would talk about work: 'My supervisor Janet Daly's a real nightmare.' Sometimes they watched television. Or they would make love.

Finally, *finally*—she had reached America.

Prema celebrated her first Thanksgiving that year. Luis's mother and stepfather Ron invited them to their home in San Diego.

Peggy Furgal, previously Peggy Reyes, born Peggy Baker.

'What is she like?' Prema asked Luis on the drive south.

'Ah, she's great—a real hippie chick.'

'Pardon?'

'You're going to get along great.'

Peggy and her husband Ron lived in a gated community of pink houses overlooking other gated communities of pink houses. Peggy met them at the front door, dressed in a tie 'n' dye outfit and bangles. Her hair was golden and her face bronze. 'Oh, darling,' she gushed, hugging Luis and kissing him on both cheeks. 'Darling, darling.' She hugged Prema: 'How wonderful to meet you at last. Welcome. Come on in.' Then she joined her palms together and bowed to Prema: 'Nah-mass-tay. I salute the god within you.'

Prema returned an awkward, off-protocol namaste: the

younger person was supposed to greet the elder first, not the other way around.

'You both look,' Peggy examined them, 'luminescent in love!'

Luis's entire family was there: his stepbrother Ryan and his wife Anna, both so wan their brows vanished into their skin. Their three sons were tearing around the living room. Anna clapped her hands to get their attention: 'Boys! Matt, Mike, Mark, meet Uncle Luis's girlfriend, Prema.'

'Hi.' 'Hi.' 'Hi.'

'Hello.'

Everyone was extremely welcoming. Ron greeted Prema with a white drink: 'Have some eggnog! I'm not ashamed to say it's my favourite part of the holiday season.'

'Oh, Ron,' Peggy said, 'don't push that on her. Wouldn't you prefer champagne, Prema darling?'

'Let her try,' Ron said. 'Do you drink eggnog back home, Prema? Try it.'

'Thank you.' She took a sip. It was repulsive.

'It's my favourite!'

Prema discovered, that day, that Luis called his mother by her name: 'So how's it going with you, Peggy?' 'You guys planning to go to that retreat in Albuquerque, Peggy?' 'Peggy, would you like some more champagne?'

The meal, when it was served, was a festive overabundance: turkey with something called stuffing, and mashed potatoes, sweet potatoes, sautéed green beans, stuffed eggplant, and an array of gravies, sauces, jellies and chutneys. Luis, seated next to Prema, kept an arm around her throughout. Everyone bantered over the meal: 'Grandma, do I have to eat everything on my plate?' 'I told you not to call me grandma, darling.' 'Mark, I told you not to use your hands.' 'Ron, you're not thinking of buying any more?' 'Too late! The prices are astronomical!' 'Prema, darling, have more bubbly.' 'Thank you.'

It was all so light of spirit.

Prema was touched to be included in the celebration of an American festival. After dinner, over coffee and a pie made of pumpkin, Luis and she, and Ryan and Anna, pored over family albums. Luis groaned at a photograph of him and Ryan as boys: 'We were such geeks!' 'I think it's adorable,' Anna said. Ryan pointed at a photograph of a teenaged Luis at a beach: 'Remember those surfer dudes? They'd go to Hawai'i for competitions! Man, they were something else.'

'More coffee, darlings?'

The gathering broke up late, with hugs all around, and promises to meet soon, promises that no one would be able to keep, but which nevertheless rang warm and sincere. At the door Peggy hugged Prema, Ron hugged Prema, Ryan hugged Prema, Anna hugged Prema. Americans hugged so much. Prema hugged Matt, Mike and Mark. Peggy gave Prema another off-protocol namaste: 'I salute the god within you.' To Luis she said, slurring on champagne, 'Oh, darling, I'm so happy you've found love again.' She planted lipsticky kisses on both his cheeks. 'You two look absolutely wonderful together,' she said. 'You deserve all the happiness in the world, darling. You too, Prema. Young people everywhere!' She hiccupped. 'You all deserve to be happy!'

'They are so nice,' Prema said on the drive back. 'They are all really so nice.'

'Didn't I tell you?'

'Really.'

'I knew you'd get along.'

'You call your mother Peggy,' she remarked.

'Yeah, Mom wasn't into hierarchy, wanted me to treat her as an equal. It's a—it's a hippie thing.'

'You also called your father Carl?'

'Oh, no, no. Dad wasn't like that at all.' Luis laughed. 'He preferred to be called Dad.'

Carl Reyes. 'What was he like?' she asked. Had he also been light of spirit? Would he have fitted into this gathering? Or was he different? Foreign? That was what Prema wanted to know.

'I've got some photos of him at home, I'll show you,' Luis said. 'They were real opposites, Mom and Dad. Dad was more—I don't know, *proper*—even though Mom was the one who came from a posh background. Her family were real WASPs. Know what a WASP is?' he asked, quickly following with, 'Not the insect kind. Mom's family was from back East, real proper folks off the Mayflower.' He digressed awhile, telling Prema about the Pilgrims. Then he returned to his mother: 'She came to study at Mills, and fell for Dad. He was slacking off, doing odd jobs even though he had an engineering degree. Her folks were horrified—but she was a wild child, Mom. Wilder than Dad, I guess. She fell for Ron when I was in middle school. Ron was a friend of Dad's.' He laughed. 'Ryan? We were friends in school, then suddenly we're stepbrothers. It was so Brady Bunch!' Then he told her about the television show.

At home, Luis showed Prema an album of photographs of his father, all crackly with age, the colours washed out and faded.

Carl Reyes had had black hair and a lean face with dark, deep-set eyes.

In one photograph he was standing on a sidewalk, somewhere urban, though Luis did not know where. 'Maybe San Antonio? That's where he lived when he first came to America. He had an uncle there.'

In another photograph, Carl was seated at a table for two, at a restaurant. 'Mom took that picture when they were just dating.'

There was another photograph of Carl by a bridge. 'That must have been when he was twenty, twenty-one. That's San Antonio. I went with Dad once, as a kid.'

There was only one photograph from before Carl came to America. In it, he was standing in front of a Spanish-style villa, squinting into the sun.

'That was taken in San Juan Cotzal, that's where Dad's family was from,' Luis said. 'He got his engineering degree in Mexico City, then went back for a couple of years. He was still Carlos Reyes-Garcia then, switched to Carl Reyes when he came here. Doesn't he look—cool?' He lingered over that photograph. 'He was such a cool cat, was Dad.'

Back at work the next day, Prema went to the library by the boat harbour to pick up a new large-print romance for Esther. As an afterthought, she checked the stacks for books on Guatemala. And saw that there were books on the rise and fall of the Maya kingdoms, and also on contemporary events. The war.

Nothing Happened

~

That Christmas, Luis's ex-wife Tina and her husband Christopher invited them for vegetarian potluck, saying that it might be good for July if everyone celebrated the festival together. Luis's closest friends, Steve and Camilla, would also be coming.

At first, Luis was not keen. 'He's a real dork,' he said about Christopher. 'Know what a dork is? It's just—a dork. He has this really naff rat-tail. And he speaks real slo-o-ow, like he's enlightened or something. Our meditation guru! You know?' But in the end he decided that for July's sake, it might be best to go: 'I guess we should try and get along, like grown-ups.' He sighed.

Luis had to work right up to Christmas Day, as Meadowvale's Head of Human Resources, a man called Sonny McGirk, quit abruptly to join a rival nursing home, throwing the administration into disarray. Luis's supervisor, Janet Daly, asked him to fill in temporarily. 'I was thinking, if there's an opening, I should apply for the job,' Luis said to Prema, explaining why he had agreed.

Prema also worked till Christmas Day, because Natalie begged her to: 'I know it's asking for a lot, it's just that I'm planning on going to Maui,' Natalie said, in what was their longest conversation since the initial job interview. 'I keep telling Dad, we should upgrade Nana to Live-in Independence and move her into Meadowvale. It's such a hassle for me, but he won't—' She frowned. 'I've already bought the plane tickets, you see. Mercury will come in on Christmas Day, but the other days—Prema, I'll pay you overtime and a half!'

It rained heavily that winter, dense showers pouring from charcoal clouds, confining Esther indoors. There were mudslides up and down the coast. 'No outings to the beach for us,' the old lady looked out the window with furrowed brows. But to Prema the rain felt like monsoon.

One afternoon, she bicycled in the rain to a shop near the boat harbour, and bought Luis a Christmas present: two Nuclear Energy CDs. It turned out that he had also got her a present. He gave it to her on Christmas morning: a handspun dress made in Nepal: 'Found it at a shop in the Galleria, believe it?'

The dress hung shapelessly on her, like a sack, but she wore it to Tina and Christopher's. Luis cooked something called paella for the potluck: 'My specialty. It's not usually vegetarian, I'll make you a proper one sometime, with chicken and shrimp and chorizo.' Prema made black daal in the Nepali style, though without an iron pot it came out brown, not black, and the main herb, jimbu, was missing.

Tina and Christopher's house in the valley stood on a quiet, oak-lined street. There was a yin-yang sign above the door, and Tibetan prayer flags up front.

July answered the door dressed all in black, her face powdered white and her eyes lined heavily with kohl.

Luis was startled. 'What happened to you?'

She rolled her eyes. 'It's called going goth, Dad!'

Tina came to the door. She was a petite, sculptured woman with a flawlessly made-up face and red drop earrings that sparkled when she moved. Her dress was of silk, tailor-fitted. Prema immediately felt like a peasant in her handspun dress.

'Hey, Luis.' The two hugged cautiously, as if just for show. Then Tina hugged Prema, all bony clavicles. 'Prema? It's wonderful to meet you. Can I take that for you?' She reached for the daal. 'Come in, please.'

When she turned, they saw a tattoo on her shoulder blade: OM. Prema thought she saw Luis flinch.

'Steve and Cami are bringing beer,' Tina said. For Prema's benefit, she explained, 'Christopher and I don't drink. Christopher's still in the kitchen,' she said. 'He's trying out a new recipe, Thai, but the tofu's breaking, so he's a bit, um, preoccupied.'

Christopher came out to greet them, a sallow man with aggrieved features, not what Prema had expected of a meditation guru. 'Luis, man. So good of you to come,' he said glumly. 'Prema? Welcome to our home. We're...honoured.' Then he turned to Tina with a scowl: 'The goddamned tofu, honey. We should have bought the other brand. The package *explicitly* said it wouldn't break. But—whoa-ho! Does the package tell the truth?' He bellowed out his own answer: 'No-o-o-o!'

Tina smiled brightly at everyone. 'Would anyone like fresh guava juice?'

Luis said he would wait for the beer. Prema said yes. Tina went off to get the juice. Christopher took Luis's paella and followed his wife to the kitchen, offering a view of his rat-tail as he left.

Luis shot Prema a look, then put an arm around July: 'So,

young lady. You know how long goth's been around? It was around when I was in high school.'

'Was not!'

'And anyway, aren't you a bit young for this?'

'Nora's gone goth.'

'But Nora's in junior high, right?'

Tina returned in a while with the guava juice. 'The daal looks delicious,' she said to Prema, nodding. Her drop earrings sparkled. 'Do you mind if I ask if it has any dairy?'

'Pardon?'

Luis answered for her. 'It's got butter. So does the paella. Why? Oh, don't tell me you've gone vegan!'

'No, not me,' she said.

In the silence that followed Prema could almost hear what everyone was thinking.

The atmosphere eased when Steve and Camilla arrived.

'Yo, man, it's been too long!' Steve hugged Luis like a long-lost brother. Camilla, too, gave him a long hug: 'Oh, Luis! ¡Usted parece muy, muy atractivo! It's so great to see you!' Luis introduced them to Prema. Then: 'Party!' Steve began to pass around the beer.

Luis quickly finished one bottle and started on another. Camilla went to the kitchen to help Christopher. In the manner of a proper hostess, Tina kept the conversation going by plying Prema with questions:

'I was reading, there's been some trouble in Nepal? There was something in the papers a few weeks ago. Is everything all right?'

'Oh,' Prema said. 'I do not know.'

Tina nodded. Her drop earrings sparkled. 'I have a student in my yoga class,' she said, 'in the beginner's level. She gives money to an orphanage in Nepal. She's been there lots of times, really loves the country. She says the Nepalese are very—' She paused. 'They might not have much by way of material possessions, but they're spiritually rich.'

Prema could find no response to this.

Tina reached over to feel her handspun dress: 'I just love this! Is it from Nepal? Is this the kind of dress the Nepalese wear?'

Prema thought of all the regional outfits that people wore all over the country, and said, inarticulately, 'We wear different-different things.'

Tina nodded earnestly.

'So,' Luis cut in, 'Christopher's gone vegan?'

'He feels it helps unblock the chi,' Tina said.

'Oh, what, his chi got blocked?'

Steve intervened: 'Beer unblocks the chi! More beer, anyone?'

Luis took another bottle. Prema also switched to beer. Tina sipped primly at her guava juice. Christopher's daughter Nora joined them eventually, a teen, sallow like her father, and outfitted, like July, in black goth robes. Ignoring Tina's look of disapproval, she helped herself to a beer.

Christopher and Camilla laid out the dinner: a smattering of Thai vegetables with broken tofu, paella, black daal, roasted beets and peppers, yams, asparagus, sprouts and raw vegetables. Before eating, Christopher made everyone form a circle and pray. Prema held his big, clammy hand and Camilla's warm, small hand. Then Christopher slowly intoned: 'Bless this food, oh…Krishna, Allah, Yahweh, Gaia…that nourishes our bodies and…spirits. We pray.' He paused. 'That all souls everywhere obtain. Nourishment. And may there be…peace. For…our brothers and sisters. In…Iraq, Afghanistan, and Abu Ghraib.' He sighed. 'May our leaders make. Wiser policies. Help America. Become more…compassionate. Elect a Democrat. In the next. Election. Save the planet from. Environmental destruction. End the war. Close Guantanámo. Heal the world. Jai. Guru. Dev.' At the end he smiled at everyone, one by one. 'Merry Christmas,' he said. 'Thank you for coming to our humble home. Merry Christmas. Merry Christmas. Merry Christmas.'

'Merry Christmas.'

'Merry Christmas.'

'Wine?' Steve poured it out into glasses.

Soon, everyone except the hosts had had too much to drink. Was it the alcohol? Prema was unable to keep up as the conversation grew animated, topics tossed back and forth so blithely. Camilla told everyone she was going to start yoga classes at the school where she taught: 'With girls that age especially, there's so much anxiety around the body.' 'Hey, you know what's become real big?' Steve said: 'Water jogging!' 'Yeah, everyone who was doing yoga and Pilates has moved on to that,' Tina said. Luis laughed: 'And water ballet!' He told everyone there might be an opening for Head of Human Resources at Meadowvale. 'Go for it, man,' Steve said. Tina talked about an advanced yoga intensive she was teaching: 'It really flushes out the lymphatic system.' Then Christopher got talking about his guru, a woman called Mata Sylvia who taught at a temple in Inglewood. She had spent years in the Himalayas, he said. 'She's. The. Best,' he said. 'Simply. The. Best.'

It was then—nothing happened, nothing at all— Just, as Prema was listening to them, these…Americans: Tina and Christopher—she did not know their surnames—and Steve

Adams and Camilla Arguelles, and Luis, Luis Reyes, something jarred in her, a question. She wondered: why were Americans so light of spirit?

Why should they not be?

After dinner, Nora and July went upstairs to watch a video. Christopher brought out a pipe. He lit it, took a puff, and passed it to Steve, who was talking about a weekend he and Luis had taken to Las Vegas, two years back. 'I thought we'd make a killing on the blackjack tables,' Steve was saying, 'but our man here spends all his time at the fucking slot machines! I'm trying to drag him away. Money, money?' Steve took a puff of the pipe and offered it to the others, who declined. When he exhaled Prema recognized the smell of marijuana. 'But Luis is just waiting for the quarters to go ka-ching, ka-ching!'

'I was not!' Luis protested.

'It's good to be cautious,' Camilla said thoughtfully.

'The boy wasn't being cautious, Cami, he was draining all his money into the fucking slot machines!'

'Bullshit, man!'

'Ka-ching!'

All so light of spirit.

Camilla announced: 'Sorbet for dessert! Raspberry, I made it myself!'

'Oh, yum!' Tina passed the bowls around, and everyone started, again, to talk.

'It's okay, it's okay to like slot machines!'

'I don't like slot machines!'

'You love them, man.'

Camilla turned to Luis. 'Estaba bromeando.'

'Sí, lo sé,' he replied, laughing.

She turned to Prema. 'Would you like more sorbet, Prema?'

'No, thank you.'

She turned back to Luis. '¿Quieres mas helado?'

'No. Estoy muy gordo,' he said.

'¡Yo no! ¡El helado no engorda!'

'Okay, pero no mucho.' He held out his bowl. 'Oh, así está bien,' he said. '¡Asi está bien!'

Heading back, Luis took a winding canyon road. He was in an expansive mood now: 'I wasn't sure when Tina suggested it, but it worked out okay, don't you think? It's good for July to see her parents getting along. And— I don't think Tina's happy with the dork, she seems so—rigid. Tight. But she's a big girl, I guess. What's with the rat-tail, though!'

'That was marijuana,' Prema remarked.

'Yeah, looks like the guru's a bit of a toker. Steve's always been.'

'Camilla,' Prema said. 'She is—Latino?'

'Latin*a*. Chicana, actually: Mexican-American. Her full name is something like Camilla Ramona Barrera Morales something-something-something Arguelles.'

'Steve is also Chicana?'

'Chican*o*. No, he isn't, he's a good old-fashioned white boy.'

'A WASP like your mother?' It occurred to Prema to ask: 'All white people are WASPs?'

'No, no. Like my stepdad, Ron? He's Polish.'

'I thought Ron was American.'

'I mean Polish-American. And Anna? She's Irish-American.'

'How can you tell who is Irish-American and who is Polish-American?' Prema asked.

Luis laughed. 'You mean 'cause all white folks look the same?' Then he explained, 'Sometimes someone might look typically Irish, or typically Polish, or their name gives it away. But other times you can't tell unless you know their background.'

'What kind of white person is Steve?' Prema asked.

'Well, not everyone cares, also, about their— And people are of mixed backgrounds sometimes.' He said, 'I think Steve's from the Midwest, he's probably Lutheran or something, but I don't really know.'

'What kind of white person is Christopher?'

'Christopher's a hundred per cent white trash.'

'What kind of white person is Esther?'

'I'm pretty sure she's Jewish, but you could ask her. Not in those words, of course.' He looked over. 'And Prema: white trash? That's not an expression you should use. I don't actually know what kind of white person Christopher is. He's just a dork is what he is.'

'Americans are confusing,' Prema said.

He laughed.

She watched him laugh. 'And what are you?' she asked. 'You are—half-Latino?'

'You mean, like, what's my *identity*? Half WASP, half Guatemalan-American, I guess. Or half Centro-Americano, whatever. Now everyone just says Latino. I was more interested in that stuff in college—guess I had the time, then, to think about stuff like that. Latinidad: the Latino takeover of America. We were all big into that.'

Prema was still trying to think through all this. 'If you are half Guatemalan-American, and Tina is Chinese-American, this makes July…what?'

'Tina and I used to talk about that,' Luis said. 'July Chan-Reyes—she's half Chinese-American, and from my side—what? A quarter WASP, a quarter Latina. A mutt.'

Prema mused over this. Outside the windshield, the metropolis was a blur of light and dark. 'Your father called himself Guatemalan-American?' she asked.

'Nah. The Chicano rights movement was big when Dad came here, but the problem was, he wasn't Mexican. And you know what Americans are like. When he told people he was Central American, they'd be like, "Oh, you're from Brazil?" I think Dad wasn't into labels,' he said. 'It was a different era. People wanted to assimilate. He was into being—American, you know?'

She thought about how often she was taken for Latino—Latina. She said, 'Teach me some Spanish, Luis.'

He laughed. 'No soy Mexicana?'

'Something else.'

'Soy muy, muy atractiva? Or how's this.' He put on a mock-seductive voice and ran a hand up her thigh: 'Quiero hacer el amor contigo.'

'I am serious.'

He shrugged. 'The thing is, I'm kind of into all this, and I'm kind of not, you know? I mean, ultimately we're all one, right? And I was raised a bit—well, Spanish wasn't part of my home life, I didn't speak it with Dad, had to learn it later, in school.' He said, 'For you, though, señorita. Nepalese, sorry, Nepali, is your mother tongue. You should teach me some.'

It was Prema's turn to laugh.

'Try me,' he said. 'It's the same script as Saanz-kreet, right? Day-va-na-ga-ree?'

Just the way he pronounced it made her smile. 'All right.' Slowly, she said: 'Ka, khha, ga, ghha, nga.'

'Come again?'

'The first five letters of the alphabets. Ka, khha, ga, ghha, nga.'

'Um.' He said, 'Ka, ka, ka, ka, ka.'

She laughed.

'Say it again. Say it slower this time.'

'Ka.' Pause. 'Khha.' Pause. 'Ga.' Pause. 'Ghha.' Pause. 'Nga.'

'You're toying with me,' he said. 'You're going ka ka ka ka ka to make a fool out of me!'

'I am not, I am not,' she said. 'Just try.'

'Ka. Ka. Ka. Ka. Ka.'

She burst out laughing.

'That's what you said!' he cried. 'That's exactly what you said!'

'Ka-ka-ka-ka-ka!' She laughed.

He started to laugh too. 'Ka-ka-ka-ka-ka!'

'Ka-ka-ka-ka-ka!' She laughed.

'Ka-ka-ka-ka-ka!'

The Migration of Carlos Reyes-Garcia

~

The question that had jarred Prema's mind remained, though. Why were Americans so light of spirit? The next time she was at the library by the boat harbour, she looked up a few of the books on Guatemala. Trying to get the feel of Carl Reyes. For he would have been different. A foreigner. He would have known of the world's sorrows.

He would have been born when? In the mid-1940s. This had been a hopeful time in Guatemala: the start of democratic rule. Ten Years of Spring. By the 1950s, though, business and military interests had grown alarmed at the populist—Leftist—policies of the elected government. Prema learned that with the backing of the CIA, a deposed colonel had launched a coup from Honduras, a coup nicknamed Operation PBSUCCESS. After having succeeded in overthrowing the elected government, the colonel himself had been assassinated. Another army officer had come to power. But then younger army officers had mounted another rebellion; and this had launched thirty-six years of civil war.

Nunca mas.

Prema had not known about any of this.

'Did you know?' she asked Luis that evening. 'The CIA

supported the overthrow of the democratic government of Guatemala. The CIA said the civilian government was communist, but it was not.'

'Yeah, makes you feel great about Uncle Sam, huh?'

She asked Luis more about his father, and he obliged:

Carl Reyes had grown up in San Juan Cotzal, and later, gone to Mexico City to study engineering. This was in the mid-1960s. Then he had returned home. Luis wasn't sure what he had done for work. 'He stayed a couple of years.' He had come to America in 1968, aged twenty-three. 'He bummed around for a couple of years in San Antonio, then came to San Diego and stayed on.'

He had kept in touch with his family, but had never gone back. Luis remembered sending postcards to his grandparents when he was in kindergarten. 'Dear Abuelito, dear Abuelita, how are you in Guatemala? I'm fine in America—that kind of thing.' He laughed. He said, 'I don't think that area was as badly hit by the war as Guatemala City or the areas farther out: the highlands. Dad had a couple of older sisters. One was a teacher in Guatemala City. The other one married a businessman in Mexico City. Both my grandparents died when I was young. Abuelito went first, a heart attack. I remember Dad telling me a few years later that Abuelita had also died. I don't remember—Oh, yeah. Pneumonia.'

'Your father did not go back for their funeral, even?' Prema asked.

'No, he didn't,' Luis said.

'He never went back?'

'Not that I know of, after I was born. No, actually. Never.'

'That was all right?' she said.

He shrugged. 'Guess he got caught up in his life here. Once he got the job at the Department of Public Works he stopped slacking off. He worked really hard. And when he wasn't working he was playing chess. Competed in championships and everything. He was ranked pretty high.'

'What did he think about the war?' Prema asked.

'Dunno. He never talked about it, and I guess I was your typical self-absorbed kid. I never asked about his life outside of family. But my sense is? He just wanted to—get on with life, you know.'

Yes, she thought. She knew.

Yet— There are aspects to us that originate in things impersonal, things we are part of by association. Things that claim us.

Carlos. Carl. Prema. Premma. Prima. Pray-muh.

Each time Prema returned to the library she looked up more on Guatemala. She learned that through the 1970s, rebel groups—some pacifist, others advocating armed revolution—had been organized in the countryside, and, when the army broke them there, they attacked the capital. To counter them, a series of militarized governments had led a brutal counter-insurgency in the 1980s. Atrocities had escalated as the government set vigilantes and death squads loose on peasants and Leftist intellectuals. The American government had supplied military aid for all this, save for a brief arms embargo imposed by Jimmy Carter. Ronald Reagan had lifted the embargo even as General José Efraín Ríos Montt had escalated the counter-insurgency to genocide: people had been lined up and shot, hacked down with machetes, burned to death, tortured. Eyes gouged out, tongues cut, ears cut, limbs hacked—buried alive, tossed into mass graves amid corn fields and orchards, in wayside gulches. The land had been littered with skeletons still clothed, rope-bound bones, cloth-covering on their mouths, tibia, femurs covered with earth…

'Did you know?' Prema asked Luis.

'Yeah,' he said. 'I mean, yeah. Of course. It's really horrible what happened.'

'I did not know,' she said, wondering what else she didn't know.

'Your father worked for the American government,' she remarked to Luis, once.

'Department of Public Works.' He smiled. 'There was one time when I was a kid, he heard me telling my friends that my dad made roads. So he took me out in his Ford to show me a junction he'd designed. He parked by the side, and pointed to the junction and said, 'When other kids ask what your dad does, don't say he makes roads. I *design* roads. There's a big difference, okay? I *design* roads.'

After getting divorced from Peggy in the mid-1980s, Carl had moved to Boulder with his girlfriend Nan. During this period Guatemalans had poured into America, seeking asylum from a war that America was supporting.

'Did your father know any refugees?' Prema asked.

'I don't think so,' Luis said. 'And, well, it wasn't like he came as a refugee himself, you know? Mostly Dad just worked. He worked so hard, I hardly saw him when I was a kid. Even later, when I visited him in Boulder— And when he wasn't working, he was playing chess. Always had six or seven games set up in his den. One of his partners lived in Dallas, another in Boston. This was before the Internet—they'd phone or write letters to make each move. Those games went on forever! You ever play chess?'

'A bit.'

'I've got one of his sets somewhere.'

The more Prema found out about Guatemala, the more she wanted to find out.

'Did you know, two hundred thousand people were killed or disappeared?' she asked one evening.

Luis looked at her. 'You're really getting into this, huh.'

'Two hundred thousand.'

'Yeah, it's awful.'

It turned out that whatever she learned, Luis already knew. None of this had affected him the way it did her. He understood her shock and was kind about her ignorance. 'It's always the ordinary people who get screwed the worst,' he explained to her once. 'The Mayas had it the worst.'

'I thought the Mayas disappeared mysteriously.'

'You mean they got beamed up in a spaceship?' He laughed. Then he explained: 'Los Indios: the Q'anjob'al, other tribes. The old Maya kingdoms collapsed, but it's the same people. The indigenous people. Dad wasn't— His family was ladino, of Spanish descent. He wasn't really in touch with indigenous culture. But it's an amazing, rich—' He said, 'There's this Mayan saying, in lak ech. Tú eres mi otro yo: you are my other me. I remember thinking, in college—*exactly.* That's exactly right.'

Another time, Luis told her about the refugees in LA. 'When I was in college you'd see them selling fruit and vegetables, or flowers, by the side of the road. Everywhere. You couldn't miss them.'

Prema said, 'It must be strange to come to a country that is supporting the war that they are running away from.'

'Well, America's also the land of opportunity, right? I mean, look, things are complicated. And America's changing. We've had a Latino mayor, and who knows? We might even have a black president one day. Though that may be asking for too much—'

'But it must be strange.'

'Yeah, sure. It's still not easy. Some got involved in gangs and drugs and stuff, now they're like the biggest gangs. You heard of the maras, like Mara Eighteen? The American government deported them, sent them to Guatemala City, so now they've got the same gangs there that we have in LA!'

'There are gangs in LA?'

He gave her a look. 'Um. Not where we live, but yeah.'

What puzzled Prema was how all this had happened—how Americans seemed to know this had happened—yet this knowledge did not weigh them down. Had life in Guatemala ever returned to normal? On a day-to-day basis, more people were being murdered there in crime-related violence now than had been by war. The 1990s peace process had not ended the violence; it had only altered its form: the profiteers of war had turned to organized crime.

'They are all in gangs?' she asked Luis a few days later.

'What?'

'The Guatemalans are all in gangs here?'

'No, god, no. It's just a few bad eggs. The rest—I mean, it's just ordinary people, right? When they got here they needed jobs but didn't know the language and couldn't find anything, so they were working in factories, living piled up in a few rooms in the seedy parts. I can't imagine—leave your country, your whole life, and set up somewhere new.'

'What does seedy mean?' she asked.

'Seedy? Um, like run-down. Why?'

'You said seedy.'

'Did I? Yeah, run-down. Grubby, you know?' He said, 'Lots of Guatemaltecos are still working in factories, or as maids, in low-paying jobs. You come to this country thinking you're going to have a better life, and it turns out you're living in places that most of the locals are too scared to live in. You have to lock yourself in all night just to stay safe. Then the gangs start moving in, recruiting the kids. It must be awful.'

'Was the street I lived in before seedy?' Prema asked. 'With Meg and Susan. Was that seedy?'

'A bit,' Luis said cautiously.

'Can we go there?' she asked. 'Where they live?'

'Where the Guatemaltecos live?' He laughed; she was hurt. He noticed. 'Of course,' he said. 'Yeah, of course, definitely we could do that, definitely. Though—' He added, 'It's not like there's anything to see. It's just...where they live, you know?' Then he said, 'Though maybe I could find something. A concert or a market or something.'

¿Cómo Ha Dicho?

~

Luis decided it would be best to attend a church service in a Guatemalan neighbourhood. The following Sunday, over breakfast, he pored over the listings in the newspapers. July was with them that weekend. She had given up her black goth robes for provocatively short dresses. She and Luis had been arguing about this all morning.

'It's just a style, Dad,' she was saying. 'It's called Lolita. Nora says it's big in Japan.'

'Yeah, and you know what kind of people like girls called Lolita?'

There were several kinds of services listed in the newspapers: Catholic, Charismatic Christian, Protestant. 'Listen to this.' Luis read aloud: 'Assembly of God. Christian Fellowship. Cathedral of Life. Eternal Light Church. Missionary Baptist. Hope Chapel. Community Church. Church of God.'

'Um. Why are you guys going to a church, anyway?' July asked.

'Nothing wrong with going to church on Sunday morning. Want to come?'

'Do I have to?'

'Jim and Berry said you could have lunch with Gemma.'

'Phew!'

'Church of Religious Science, Faith Center, St. Joseph Church,' Luis read aloud. 'The Journey Church. Hey, I like that: the Journey Church. And the New Hope Center. Oh, and Our Lady of Guadalupe.'

The church he selected was downtown. After dropping July off at Jim and Berry's, they took the 110 north, reaching the skyscrapers just past eleven. There were no parking spaces by the church, so Luis looped back to a street by a green park, a park with palm trees and a pond. MacArthur Park. Where Prema had been to the Salvadorian street fair.

'We're late.' Luis led her through the untidy—seedy?—clutter of groaning old buildings: Upper Mind Church Daily Donut Smoothie JESUS S VES Cappuccino. They passed the stately building that she had gone into, back when she had wanted, so badly, to reach America. Skirting a drunk on the pavement they passed the Money Gram Family Market, Pedro's Electronics, Maria's Comida Salvadoreña. The church was in a concrete-block building with a sign—MINISTERIO CRISTIANO—up front.

Through a door they entered a dark cavern fragrant with burned juniper. They stood awhile to let their eyes adjust to the darkness. Inside, there was foot-scraping, shuffling and fidgeting, whispering. Low-watt bulbs flickered on the walls. Slowly, Prema made out a hall full of people seated on benches. A cross loomed over an altar, backlit, afloat in ultramarine. There were some people at the altar, but she could not make out what they were doing. It was cool in the hall. Prema shivered.

A woman came in behind them, crossed herself, and sat on a

nearby bench. Luis and Prema seated themselves next to her. Some children were whispering in the row in front of them. A man cuffed a boy, who just giggled. A woman behind them said something to the other, who suppressed a grunt of laughter.

It was roundabout, the way Prema's mind revealed itself. In that hall she looked from face to face, and realized: she had been trying to remember the war in her life by learning about the war in the lives of others.

For the first time in years, Prema really thought back to Nepal.

The war.

She thought of her father. Was he safe?

Her sister. Was Bijaya still a Maoist? Was she even alive?

She thought of Kanchha, back in the hill bazaar. Had he ever been found?

She felt an ancient shivering in the marrow.

She was lucky to have left the war in Nepal. She thought of Carl. He had not been caught up in the war in Guatemala. He had also been lucky. Luis knew war only from a distance. He was lucky too.

Though mortality, of course, follows us everywhere. She thought of her mother. Complications from childbirth. Carl Reyes. Pancreatic cancer.

In that hall, Prema thought: when an animal dies, when we say it has died, we mean that the supply of oxygen to the brain has ended, electrical activity has stopped. This can happen suddenly, as when the animal is shot fatally, or is decapitated; or it can happen gradually, as when it is wounded or made to suffer beyond physical endurance: bled to death, burned to death; internal damage or irreparable wounds inflicted to the vital organs. Pain is the body's method of alerting animals to danger. Assuming the animal is in a position to do so, heeding the pain can save its life. Sometimes it is powerless to do so—it is captive, say—and so the damage inflicted cannot be repaired. An awareness of impending death exists in humans. At the moment of death, psychologically, the easiest way to die is to lack foreknowledge of one's death, to be spared that knowledge. The most difficult thing is to know that one is going to die. Here, now.

She shivered. Difficult enough to die naturally. But to be killed— To know that one was going to be killed.

A thickset man came to sit beside her on the bench. He was muttering—prayers?—under his breath. At the altar, someone said something in Spanish. Then everyone stood and recited prayers, the hall rumbling with voices.

That brought the service to a close. Afterwards, some people left. Others lingered, gathering in small groups to talk. For a while Luis and Prema just stood there. The children who had been whispering earlier now ran out of the church, giggling. The woman who had earlier grunted in laughter was now talking animatedly with her friend. The thickset man beside Prema was still muttering under his breath. He had a hunch to his shoulders, his eyes were almost closed, and he looked asleep, standing. Only his lips were moving. He took in a deep breath, exhaled, and looked at Prema, his eyes watchful and uneasy.

It was the middleman. His thickset build, his watchful manners. The middleman from the town at the base of the hills.

It couldn't be.

'Shall we go?' Luis asked.

The middleman leered at her.

'Shall we go?' Luis asked again.

Prema nodded. Her heart was pounding. She felt paralysed. With an effort, she shuffled past the middleman. Then, as Luis walked on, she turned back in one fierce instant, whispering: 'Tapaain kahaanbaata yahaan aaipugnubhaeko?'

The middleman kept leering.

'Kahaanbaata yahaan aaipugnubhaeko?' she repeated.

The middleman coughed. His eyes darted.

'Tapaain Harihar Bohora haina? Harihar Bohora haina? Kahaanbaata yahaan—?'

'¿Cómo ha dicho?' the man said. 'Lo siento, señorita. No hablo Inglés.'

Of course. Prema reeled. Of course it was not him.

She careened past him and out the hall, knocking past people at the door, stumbling unsteadily on to the sun-blinded pavement.

'Hey.' Luis put an arm around her. 'Thought I lost you there. I've got an idea.'

She tried to calm herself. 'What?'

He looked at her. 'You okay?'

'Yes. Yes. What idea?' she said.

'I saw a place we could have lunch.'

Maria's Comida Salvadoreña was a diner with three plastic foldaway tables and no decorations except for a wind chime at the door. At the counter a matron was reading a newspaper, *El Chapin USA*. Behind her, a young woman clattered about an open kitchen. Luis and Prema ordered chille relleno and carne guisada from the matron, and paid up front.

'So, Prema?' Luis said after they were seated at one of the foldaway tables. 'They announced the opening for Head of Human Resources last week.' He looked out the window at an abandoned warehouse, lost in thought. Then he turned back. 'The board's going to prioritize in-house applications, and I've been filling in all these months, so I was thinking my chances are good. Though it means I'd be doing a lot more paperwork.' He let out a laugh. 'It all comes down to shuffling paper in my line of work. I think I'd have a good shot at this job. The only thing is, it's management level.'

He explained that it would be a significant promotion. 'They've never hired anyone like me in management. I mean, I started as concierge, right? They've never had anyone like me move up that high.'

'Is it a job you will like?' Prema asked.

'Well, the money's good.'

Upon divorcing, Tina and he had sold the house that they had bought together. He had invested his share in the down payment for his flat, which had cost half a million, he said.

'Half what?' Prema asked, incredulous.

'Yeah, the prices are crazy. Half a million.'

'Dollars?'

He laughed: 'Yeah, what else? Dollars.'

Right now, most of his salary went towards the mortgage payment, he said. There was child support. The Saturn was paid for, but there was car insurance. And health insurance: though Meadowvale covered most of the costs, he paid out of his pocket for eye and dental. The coverage for July was limited. 'Every month, after paying all the fees, bills and credit card expenses, there's nothing left.'

The matron brought them two plates with gravy-smeared chicken, and buttery beans with rice.

'¡Tiene buena pinta!' Luis said.

She nodded. '¡Que aproveche!'

'Looks pretty much like Mexican food,' he said after the matron left. 'Maybe it is a little different. I can't tell. A little heavy on the butter.' Then he asked, 'So, you think I should apply for the job?'

He clearly wanted to do so. She said yes.

He looked relieved. 'Me too. I think I should at least try.'

She was feeling better now; the mix-up at the church was behind her. The diner felt comforting somehow. It felt familiar. At one point a man came in, lean and rangy, in oil-stained overalls. Without being asked, the matron brought him a bowl of soup. He stooped over it at once. By and by, two other men came in, and stood at the counter chatting with the matron. When the first man finished his soup, he put a five-dollar bill on the table, and left with a nod to the others.

'This is like a teashop at home,' Prema said to Luis. 'You go and order and pay. If there is somebody there, you talk. If not, you drink your tea and leave. It is just like this—seedy?'

'No-frills.'

'Luis,' she said, 'the war in Guatemala is like the war at home. It reminds me of that.'

He looked at her. 'Yeah, I figured it was something like that. Are they similar, the two wars? Oh, shit,' he said. 'Did we screw Nepal too?'

'No. Yes. No. The American government gave M-16s to the army, but not so many. We are too far away. And it is two separate histories. But—' Prema tried to find her meaning.

'Guatemala's war is like—the original war. What we have is a photocopy war. Not exactly, but there are similarities— Luis,' she said, wanting to tell him about so much. But the only words that came to her were, 'People can be so evil.'

'Yeah, they really can be animals.'

'But animals are not evil. Only humans are.'

The matron came and offered them seconds.

'Para mí no, gracias,' Luis said.

Prema said no, thank you.

'¿Ustedes son Salvadoreños?' the matron asked.

Luis replied, 'Mi padre era Guatemalteco.'

'Si, paraces ladino. ¿Y ella?'

'Es Asiatica.'

'¡Eh! ¡Aparenta Salvadoreña!'

He laughed. '¡Sí, supongo que sí!'

Her Mother, Laughing

~

After this, Prema began to feel out of place where she was. Living in a flat on a toy street. Working as a homecare attendant. Ensconced snugly in Luis's life, his very—American—life. She hadn't actually reinvented herself, had she? She had just drifted along a zigzag trail, as always. And though there was nothing wrong with the life she had now, though she was content enough, it just— This was not really her place.

She barely got a chance to reflect on this, though, because only a few days after putting in his application, Luis discovered that his supervisor, Janet Daly, had applied for the same job as well.

'She's a nurse, I don't know what she's doing applying for a post in administration,' he told Prema. 'Sonny McGirk didn't have a medical background. You don't *need* one for this job. But Janet Daly's telling everyone that her background will be a plus.' He groaned. 'And I can see the board going for her. I mean, I've really kept the place together all these months. But they've never hired someone like me in management.'

'Do not worry,' Prema said.

'My application's strong, but— Plus Janet Daly's a woman, right? They'll go for her.'

'Do not worry, Luis.'

But he did worry. 'You don't *need* a medical background,' he would say, apropos of nothing. Unable to sleep, he would toss in bed, and get up in the middle of the night to rummage though the bathroom cupboard for pills. In the morning he would wake up groggy and have to skip meditation.

She had never seen him like this. It surprised her. But she saw, in the following weeks, that much depended on this job. There was, in Luis's mind, something inadequate about his life at present. The new job was part of a schema he was following, a schema that would direct him to the life he dreamed of, a proper and solid life. 'I was thinking,' Luis said one evening, 'the apartment's kind of small for the two of us. Real estate value is still appreciating, so it might be a good time to look around for something bigger—it's been years I've been wanting to.'

The following evening, he told her that he had looked up prices on a website called californiamoves.com. 'Just checking.' He had seen a condo listed at 800,000 on one of the smaller streets of Manhattan Beach, and on another street, another condo for a million dollars. 'I bet if we looked around we could find something cheaper, though— I'll call Tina and get the number of their agent. They got a great price for their house.' He didn't just want a new flat. He was also thinking of a new car. 'I've had the Saturn forever,' he said one evening. 'Not that I can afford anything fancy right now—the Lexus will have to wait.' He smiled. 'But there's a Honda dealership in the plaza: I was thinking I should stop by and ask about financing for a Civic.'

He did so over the weekend. After that, he was full of plans, going over the matter of monthly payments, maintenance costs, insurance premiums. 'I think it's doable,' he said. 'Once I—if I get this job, it's definitely doable. A Civic would be great.'

Then he returned to worrying: 'I really hope— You don't *need* a medical background. Sonny McGirk didn't have one!'

'It's driving me up the wall. The board still hasn't decided.'

'Please do not worry so much, Luis.'

The more clearly Prema saw the schema of his life, the more out of place she began to feel where she was. One evening, in the bathroom, she caught the view on to the plaza parking lot. The lot spanned several blocks, all vacant at that hour, the diagonal white lines resembling the abstract paintings on Esther's dining-room wall: the habitats of anteaters, kangaroos and armadillos, Esther had said. The plaza parking lot looked like the habitat of cars.

What was she doing here?

But if not here, then where *was* she meant to be?

There was nothing wrong with what she had now. She was content enough. She also *did* belong with Luis. Didn't she?

To dispel her doubt, she initiated sex later that evening. There was a spot on Luis's neck, by the vein—when she kissed it, it made his energy surge. She kissed him there. Felt his temperature rising. Lingered over the palpitations at his pulse points. And soon his thighs were flexing and flexing. She lost herself in the white sap of their vitality. They did not talk, that evening, making love. He did not say, 'She likes it,' and she did not say, 'I like it.' She did not say, 'Please,' and he did not say, 'Please what?' They just bared the other to the flesh and—fucked—so that she couldn't think, she didn't have to, she could just open herself to his thrusts, her convulsions, their pleasure, his briny explosion.

Afterwards, it was better.

Luis, too, was more reflective. 'Sometimes I think—' He said, 'I've got so much.'

'You do,' she agreed.

He looked at her, seeking affirmation. 'You know, the thing is— I'm going to make a confession, okay?' He said, 'The first time I saw the house Tina and Christopher bought together—it was so big, my first thought was: no wonder Tina left me. I'm a—a loser.'

'Luis—'

'I know it's ridiculous. Ridiculous. It's just— It's just, I keep feeling like I'm falling behind. And if I don't get this job—' He sighed. 'But then, even if I do get it—' He reached over to the bedside table for the bag of aquamarine marbles. He spilled them on to the bedcover and watched them roll helter-skelter. 'Remember, you said you used to play with marbles as a kid? That really struck me,' he said. 'The simple life. I— I need to get back to the basics. Liberate myself from the, uh, material world.' He said, 'Remember, at Christmas, Christopher was telling us about his guru, Mata Sylvia? Not that I really trust the dork, but—' He said, 'Maybe she could help me find inner peace.'

His queer practice.

There was still so much about Luis that Prema did not understand. He was so—foreign.

Would going to this Mata Sylvia give him inner peace?

And her? Would it help her regain a sense of belonging?

'I will go too,' she said.

On a Saturday morning, they left an hour early to get to Mata Sylvia's meditation class. Just north of the plaza, though, all the roads were jammed. 'Shit,' Luis said as they stalled. 'Construction.' Fifteen minutes later, they had barely inched forward. 'I should have cut across to Western or Vermont,' he muttered. 'Then I could have turned back in at Florence. If I go farther out this way it'll take longer to get back in.' He glanced at the clock on the dashboard. 'We're going to be late.'

The tension got to Prema: she felt the throb of a headache coming on.

Eventually, at a crossroads, they were able to turn off. But further on they got stalled on the hill with oil rigs. Prema looked out at the rigs. Luis's mind was on traffic: 'What's going on here?' They inched down the hill and entered a sprawl of low-income houses. There they saw a shop with a giant yellow doughnut on the roof. Prema recognized it from one of her early bus rides from Little Nepal.

'Look!' she said.

'God, it's ugly!'

For some reason this hurt her.

Just then he put on the traffic report: 'Folks, bad news if you're heading west…'

'Do we have to listen to this?' she snapped.

'Huh? No. Here.' He fiddled with the dials, to tune into another radio station. But every time he got a signal he moved on: 'That's eighties retro; that's Steve's easy listening station; that's hip hop; that's a loony Christer…'

At last, they pulled up at a house with a small signboard: The Society for Universal Transcendence. The neighbourhood was desolate, with not a single tree in sight. The house, as they entered, was still. Past the front door they were hit by a cloud of incense. There was a second door inside, with more incense beyond. Prema coughed. From beyond: 'Shhh.'

Inside, twenty or twenty-five people were sitting on the floor in a room with shaggy green carpeting. Everyone—save Prema—was white, though of what varieties she could not identify. Luis took a seat at the back. She sat next to him. At the very front of the room, a woman with a wizened face and milky eyes was whispering. Mata Sylvia. Mata. Mother. Her whispering was so low as to be nearly inaudible: 'And I was looking at the man who had given me such negativity.' Prema had to lean in to hear. The Mata was saying, 'And I was thinking, who is it that feels hurt? This pain: who feels it? What makes up the 'I' that I mean when I say I?'

Behind the Mata, on the wall, hung a portrait of a glint-eyed man: some Hindu guru or the other. The shelves in the room were lined with books: the Bhagavad Gita, the Mahabharat, the Ramayan, and books about Osho, Krishnamurti, Vivekananda, Ram Das, Sai Baba, Aurobindo, Maharishi Mahesh Yogi. It was the kind of place in which Prema's mother would have sought refuge.

The Mata kept whispering: 'That I is Krishna nature. It is Krishna nature that makes me feel hurt, and that makes me heal. Krishna is my lord and master, but he is also my friend, my brother, my father, my husband, my lover. My heart is awash in healing, divine love.'

Everyone was listening with half-smiles on their lips. Prema glanced at Luis. He was also half smiling.

'It's a wondrous love, not like the love you and I give to our families and friends. It's not a measured love, a calculated love, love with conditions attached. It's an absolute love, a love that washes over you like nectar, cleansing you, bathing you in its glow…'

Prema did not feel this love. Instead, she recalled her mother's bedroom shrine, crowded with the gods: Krishna, Parvati, Shiva, Laksmi, the avatar of Bishnu in a fossil. Had her mother felt the divine love that this Mata was whispering about? Had it made her feel safe? Even as her love for Prema's father made her lose her life?

She saw her mother with blankets drawn over her, a coal fire by her bedside. Unconscious. And in a flash it came to her: like her mother she had followed love. And where would it lead? What followed dating, having a relationship, having a committed relationship, and moving in together? Marriage. Childbirth.

A dread seeped through her.

Shit, as the Americans said. Shit. Damn. Goddamn. Hell. Fuck.

Eventually, the Mata instructed everyone to close their eyes, 'Just being. Not trying to do anything. Just being,' she whispered. 'It is when we are being that we see the light, that divine yellow-white light at the centre of your forehead, the source of all love.'

Prema closed her eyes. Someone from behind made a mewling, satisfied sound.

'Not looking for it, because the light is just there,' the Mata whispered. 'Seeing it. And focusing on that with about half your mind, loosely. Not tightly. Not trying to own the light. Just seeing it.'

Prema did try to see it. The field inside her eyelids was variegated enough for one spot to qualify as a light.

'Finding it. It's there, within us all. That divine light that is the source of love. Some people would call it Krishna love.'

At that, the yellow-white light dimmed in Prema's vision. And she saw her mother again, this time she saw her mother laughing. It was a memory, long forgotten, now recalled in a flash. Had she been six at the time? Seven? Returning from a game of marbles one day—those days of coveting a single blue marble—she had spied her mother by the Shiva-Parvati temple. There was a man with her. They were holding hands. It took a moment for Prema to recognize her own father. He looked different. Prema had never seen her parents touching before. She ducked behind the bamboo grove and watched as her father leaned into her mother, small and bony. This was a year before Bijaya's birth. Her mother had just had a baby, but the baby had not lived. Her father was whispering something into her mother's ear. Prema crept forward to hear. She heard him saying, 'It's not important, love.'

Her mother shook her head. 'It matters,' she said, adamantly. 'Only a son can open the gates of heaven.'

'Such superstition!'

'That's what is written.'

Prema's father sighed. He stared at her for a long while, contemplating. Then, with the fast, darting grace of a swift, a swallow, he kissed her. And Prema, from behind the bamboo grove, saw her mother laughing.

She was beautiful then, utterly transformed from the frail, sickly woman Prema remembered her as.

Prema's father held her by the waist, nuzzling her, as she, laughing, protested, 'Someone will see!'

'Who's going to see?'

'Tch!'

'No one will see.'

'Come in here,' she said, leading her husband by the hand into the Shiva-Parvati temple. Prema watched, transfixed, as she emerged in a while, radiant, laughing. In a while her father came out, also laughing.

'Open your eyes very slowly.'

The Mata switched on a CD player, and soon the room filled with harmonium wails and the tinny ching-ching of cymbals: bhajan hymns. The Mata then began to sing: 'Jaya Krishna, jaya Krishna, Radhe swami jaya jaya.'

Everyone started to clap.

Prema looked at Luis. He too was clapping.

'Jaya Krishna, jaya Krishna, Radhe swami jaya jaya. Jaya Krishna, jaya Krishna, Radhe swami jaya jaya. Jaya Krishna, jaya Krishna, Radhe swami jaya jaya.'

When the bhajan ended, Prema was the first one out the door. She stood looking at the desolate, treeless neighbourhood, till Luis came out.

'How'd you find it?' he asked.

She shrugged.

'Was that how it's done back home?' he asked as they walked to the Saturn. 'I'm glad I didn't find it too—weird. 'Cause the first time I went to a temple I found it a bit cultish.' He laughed: 'Okay, a lot cultish. But you know? I'd never gotten the point of devotion. I mean, it's crazy, right, chanting to these gods whose names I can't even remember. But there's something so healing about it.'

They drove back listening to the radio: a singer telling a woman to shake her booty if she wanted money. The sun caught a window and flashed in Prema's eyes. The car engine hummed with the velocity of them hurtling. The singer began to brag about the size of his wallet.

'Do we have to listen to this?' she said.

'Huh? No. Here.' Luis slipped in a CD: his favourite singer began to sing about someone who was not from Texas.

'Do we have to listen to anything?' she said.

He looked over at her. 'Oh. No. I just thought—I thought you liked Lyle. But no. Of course not.' He switched off the player.

The road was open; it seemed to Prema that Luis was driving too fast. Or she was just looking to quarrel. 'I do not think those Hindu gods exist,' she said. 'Do you?'

'Nah.' He laughed. 'When I say I believe in God, it's more like a spirit that I believe in. Some kind of power.'

'The Manusmriti. Do you know its message?'

'Is that part of the Bag-bad Geeta?'

'The book where it says women are—slaves. You must not listen to them, you must beat them if they disobey you. All stupid!'

'Huh.' He said, 'But there's all these amazing goddesses—'

'Goddesses? Those goddesses? If you take the good only, and forget the bad!' she cried.

'Well, every religion's got its—'

'Luis, do you *know* about the reality?' she cried. 'I told you, my mother— Do you *know*?' Unable to stop herself, she sputtered: 'She kept getting pregnant because she wanted a son! You know how many times? One baby before me, two afterwards—they all died. And she— All she wanted was a son! In Nepal they still— People still— All these stupid white people American Hindus call this Krishna love?'

'That's a bit racist,' he said.

'*I* am racist? *I* am racist?' she cried, stung.

'Reverse racism is just another form of racism. But listen—' He steered off the freeway and looped on to a side street. Slowing, he took in a deep breath. 'I'm sorry, I didn't mean you're racist. It's just— Maybe I'm being defensive about this. I was like really glad you wanted to go, and I guess I'm a bit, well, disappointed that you didn't like it. It makes me realize— Like I'm a bit insecure that because I'm American I can't be a— Not that I want to be a Hindu. It's my practice that important, and that's not about religion, it's more—spiritual.' He said, 'Discrimination's obviously been real painful to you, Prema, and I'd like to talk about it more, to know what it meant—means. But it's been a really stressful time for me, I'm feeling so much pressure about this job, so maybe I'm a bit strung out, oversensitive or whatever. I know you're coming from a very authentic point of view, and I don't want to diminish the validity of that. I guess I'm not being open to your perspective. I'll try to understand.'

With this, Prema did not know what to do.

They had reached the plaza. He pulled into a parking space and cut the engine. 'I'd really like us to let go of our anger,' he said.

'I am not angry,' she said, realizing that in fact she was.

'Kiss and make up?' He leaned over, his lips soft on hers.

When he pulled back she felt lost.

'Hey, let's make something special for dinner,' he said. 'Shall I make paella, that dish I made for Christmas? Properly this time, non-vegetarian. We'll just need to make a quick grocery run.'

It seemed to Prema as though they had been driving all day. 'Maybe let us walk?' she said.

'Walk?'

'The shop is just there.' She gestured. 'We can take the footpath.'

'It would still take, like, twenty minutes. And footpaths? They're called sidewalks. Anyway there's no—' He said, 'I don't think there's any sidewalks there.'

This left Prema feeling utterly defeated. So they drove to Gabrielino Groceries, bought supplies, and drove back to their street. Their toy street.

'Luis,' Prema asked, desperate, 'is all of America like this?'

'Like LA? Like our street? What do you mean, Prema?'

'Like—this.' She gestured about.

'God, no!' He said, 'LA is—LA. It's not like any other American city, really. It's—LA.'

Deep Dust

~

It was then that she realized she had to go: she had to set out again on her zigzag trail. But which direction was she to take this time? That, she didn't know. She thought of her movements from her present life with Luis to her life on the dry, grassy hill, and her life in Little Nepal, and her lives farther back… Her birth village, her school and college years, her years in the hill bazaar. Her attachment to Rajan. The town at the base of the hills, the bus ride to the capital. Her weeks in limbo in Kathmandu. Her flight to America. Her time in transit at the Bangkok airport. She had passed the gates for Osaka, Dubai, Paris, Ankara, Melbourne, Amsterdam. She had taken the flight to Los Angeles. She had lost her way.

The following day, at the library by the boat harbour, Prema checked the stacks for books on Mongolia. Needing to see a ger. Ghar: home.

She found books on Mongolian folklore, the art of war, Genghis Khan, the Gobi Desert.

There were books on influenza, transition from socialism, the degeneration of grasslands. Neoproterozoic to early Cambrian dinosaurs, glacial features, fossils, new leaf-rust-resistant genes in barley.

There were books on breaking the hard seed of yellow and slender serradella, steppes and basins, yellow sand, floral interchange, fugitive dust emissions, sand dune fixation, surge tectonic evolution, deep dust.

Deep dust, deep dust.

She had to go.

'How was your day?'

'Fine.'

'How's Esther doing these days?'

'Good.'

'Did you— You didn't get up to anything new?'

'No.'

'She's okay?'

'Yes.'

'Great.'

'Yes.'

That weekend, Prema stole away to the dry, grassy hill. She didn't know why she didn't tell Luis she was going there. July was staying over with them that weekend, and she and her father were going to the Cineplex. When Luis asked if Prema wanted to come along, she lied: 'Sam asked Esther to go to a seniors' chi gong class today. I said I will bring her.'

'Oh, okay.' He said, 'What time's the class? We can drop you off there.'

'Sam said he will pick me up.'

'Oh. Okay.'

As soon as he and July left the flat, Prema left too. At the plaza bus stop, she caught the No. 444. Downtown by the skyscrapers, she transferred to the No. 2. And as she reached the dishevelled boulevard, she felt transported back to the time she had moved here from Little Nepal, thinking—I have reached America.

But America just kept unfolding.

From the bus stop, she walked up the street of rickety one-storey houses with abandoned lawns and lonely front porches. She passed the house where the good-looking Latino couple used to live with their high-spirited daughters. The house of the old black lady who never went out. The adobe that Andy had renovated. She crossed over to her old house, rickety like all the others, and toothpaste-green, with three latches on the front door and iron grills at the windows.

There was no answer when she rang the bell. As she turned to leave, though, she saw Meg hurrying towards her.

'Heya, are you here for the vacancy?' Meg said without glancing at her. 'Sorry I'm late, we had an emergency at the hospital, I just couldn't get away. Glad you're here—I figured you would have left by now, I was thinking I'd call and reschedule. Anyways.' She swept past, to the door. 'Come on in.'

'Meg,' she said, 'it is me.'

Meg turned, squinting. 'Oh!'

'Prema.'

'Prima! Wow! I didn't hardly recognize you! Oh my god! Are you—?' She looked puzzled. 'Did you come about the vacancy?'

'No.'

'Oh. I guess I got you confused with the woman who called earlier.' After a moment's pause, she said, 'Hey, why don't you come in? I'll get you an iced tea.'

'I would like that.'

'What's it been—a year already?' She led Prema into the common room. 'There's a real nice woman living in your old room, Prima, but the other one's just come free, and I'd advertised— I'm a landlady now. Did I tell you—I bought the place? The landlord, remember him, Henry Little, he put it on the market and I figured I've been looking after the building long enough I should just buy it. Plus the prices are just going up and up—I hope they never drop! Anyways. Now I'm a proud homeowner.'

She went to the kitchen and came back with two glasses of iced tea.

'What happened to your brother?' Prema asked. 'He was separating from his wife when I left.'

'You remember that?' Meg smiled, pleased. 'They worked it out in the end, hammered through all the issues, ironed everything out. I'm so glad for them! For a while it was rough, though. I kept having to go, to help out. Anyways. Did I tell you? I finished my courses and I'm working full-time now. I thought nursing would be about, like, helping people, but it turns out it's just about cutting costs for the hospital, trying to save money all the time. Hey, you know Susan got married?'

'She did?'

Meg nodded. 'She met Mister Right, go figure! A lawyer from Quebec, he has the cutest accent with those long, rolling French r's! I could listen to him all day. She just moved out, that's why the vacancy. Remember all that sleeping around she was doing? I'm so glad it stopped. Luke and I broke up last year. I was pretty messed up about it for a while, I wanted to get married and have babies and all, but he just couldn't commit.

Men! I waited three years for him! He just led me on. I think he's got issues with his mother. Anyways. I'm seeing a real nice guy right now, Tony, nothing serious, we're just dating. I'm just thirty-five, so I've got time. But not that much time! I want me some babies!' Then she paused. 'So, tell me about you.'

'Me?'

'I'm sorry we never got to say goodbye,' Meg said.

Prema told her she had moved in with her boyfriend.

Meg beamed. 'Aw, I'm so happy for you, Prima! I always wondered what was going on with you. You were always so quiet and reserved, so—*Asian*, you know what I mean? Then you suddenly left. I kept wondering if it was something I said. Like was I too much of a loudmouth? Did I scare you away? I hate it when people drop out of your life, don't you? We should keep in touch, Prima. You never did teach me how to make Indian food. Let's go out for a chicken vindaloo sometime.'

'I would like that.'

At the door, they hugged like old friends.

And yet when Prema walked down the road, she thought: not here. This was not her direction.

Along the dishevelled boulevard, she headed to Korean Supplies. When she got there, she saw that the sign for the shop was there—Hangul in red and English in blue—but the doors and windows were boarded up.

To find out what had happened, she went to Wally's Beer and Wine, across the way. The pasty, red-haired man who ran it was at the counter. 'Can I help you, Miss?'

'Please can you tell me what happened to Korean Supplies?' Prema asked.

The man shrugged. 'That place? There was a robbery there last year. Nothing happened, they just cleared out the cash till and ran, but the old lady got scared and moved shop to Koreatown.' He looked closely at her. 'Didn't you used to work there?'

'You told me to look for work there, and I did.'

'Yeah, I'd see you walking by, mornings and evenings. Always looking so serious. Never came in here—not much of a drinker, I reckoned.'

'She is okay, Mrs Han Sung?'

'Last I knew she was. You'd have to go to Koreatown to find her, though—and good luck finding anyone there!'

'Thank you.'

'You have a good day, Miss.'

Not here.

She got back to the flat before Luis. 'Sorry I'm late,' he said, coming in. 'Took July for a pizza after the movie, then dropped her off at Tina's. Hey, how was the seniors' chi gong class?'

Effortlessly, Prema repeated Sam's words from a year back: 'The teacher was always saying let the chi flow. They did different-different poses. There is a pose called crane pose.'

'Sounds fun. You do it too?' he asked.

'No.'

'Oh, you should have. And Sam dropped you off afterwards?'

'Yeah,' she said. 'Yeah!'

Not here.

Momos in America

~

Two Sundays later, Prema stole away again. She had plotted this outing more carefully. She had had to muster up some courage for it. Luis was taking July shopping, and Prema told him she would rather stay home. But as soon as he left, she also left the flat.

At the plaza bus stop, she caught the No. 144 to the Artesia transit centre. There, she transferred to the No. 130. And before long, she was back in the sleepy, elm-lined neighbourhood of low, cream-coloured houses. Little Nepal.

She got off at the bus stop and walked to her old street, stopping in front of her old house.

A reedy, pleasant-faced man answered the door.

Prema guessed from his features that he was a compatriot, but just in case, she spoke in English: 'Are Neeru-didi and Sushil-bhinaju here?'

He replied in Nepali. 'They don't live here any more. But Neeru-didi will be at the restaurant if you want to meet her.' Curious, he added, 'Where are you coming from, Didi?'

For the first time in years, Prema spoke in Nepali, the language of her sorrows. 'I used to live here with them a few years ago.'

It was as though she had announced herself as a long-lost

relative. 'Eh. Won't you—?' He opened the door fully. 'Won't you come in? My wife and I just arrived a few weeks back.' He called out to his wife, 'Sarala? Eh, Sarala?'

A pretty young woman appeared at the door.

'This didi used to live here,' the husband announced.

The wife immediately said, 'Come, have tea with us.'

'No, I just came to meet Neeru-didi,' Prema said. Then, in English, she added, 'Thank you.'

'See?' the husband turned to the wife. 'Wasn't I telling you? Everyone in America says *thank you.*' He turned back to Prema and explained: 'The other day, at the grocery shop, I said *thank you* to the woman who put the food in the bag, and you know what she said to me? *Thank you*!'

They laughed.

'We didn't think this was what America would be like,' the wife ventured. 'We thought…' She looked at her husband, then at Prema. 'I've been telling my old man, let's go back.'

The husband said, 'She misses her family.'

'Why don't you come in, Didi?' the wife said. 'Have tea. Tell us what's what in this land.'

'Another time, Bahini,' Prema promised.

'Do, really,' she said. 'It would be so helpful. We've only met other compatriots who live here, we don't have any idea what it's like'—she looked past the horizon—'out there.'

'I'll come visiting,' Prema promised. They exchanged telephone numbers. Then, after a round of joke thank-yous, she left. Thinking: not here.

From there she headed to the wide boulevard, the boulevard she had once walked daily. The air here smelled faintly of tar. She passed wax myrtle, cottonwood, laurel trees. All native species. She reached the shopping complex and was stopped by the changes.

The Shalimar had been renamed The Shangrila, and its pig-pink façade had been painted over, and replaced with a bright orange front. The string of outdoor lights remained, but now there were plants along the exterior.

Inside, too, everything was different. The smell of oil had been banished by potpourri, and the dark interior had been redone: all the surfaces were now a clean white laminate.

One of the waiters—who looked like a compatriot—asked Prema: 'Table for one?'

In Nepali, she asked: 'Neeru-didi hunuhuhchha?'

'Pardon?' said the waiter.

In English, she asked for Neeru.

'There.' He pointed at the counter.

Neeru was sitting at the till that Urmila-didi's husband used to man, jotting down figures in a notebook. She looked exactly as she used to: portly, with a drawn, pinched face, big black eyeglasses and baggy kurtha-surals.

When she saw Prema, she screamed: 'Bahini!' and leaped to where Prema was standing. She hugged her fiercely. 'Where have you been all this time? We were so worried about you—didn't know if you were alive or dead! Shouldn't you have called just once to tell us that you were all right? We thought you'd had a mishap after you left us, or something bad—really bad—had happened! We were terrified!'

'I—'

Neeru would not stop screaming: 'I kept saying to your Sushil-bhinaju, why isn't she calling, surely she'll call, let's tell the police, let's go and look for her! He said you must have left America and gone home! But I kept saying, no, she would have called us to tell us, at least, that she was leaving! You just forgot about us! You selfish, selfish girl! You didn't think about us. You don't think about anyone but yourself, do you?'

'I—'

'You were like family to us! But we—we meant nothing to you!' She glared furiously.

Prema said: 'Neeru-didi, I lost my way.'

And Neeru finally let it be. She took Prema by the hand and led her to a table. 'So much has happened, I'll never get through telling you! Our boys are fully grown now, they're just like foreigners, you wouldn't know they weren't American! Our eldest is in college—and dating a girl from some place called Antigua. As black as charcoal!' She whispered: 'At first we were shocked, but—what to do? It is the human heart. We have accepted.' Then she beamed. 'Do you know I own this restaurant now? The Shangrila—you like the name? I took out a business loan from the bank. Remember that witch Urmila? I shouldn't speak badly of her; she was diagnosed with stage-four cancer. Didn't have health insurance, so she went back to India for treatment, at a hospital called Dharamsheela. Apparently it's first-class. We Nepalis, we don't like to admit it, but...those Indians have really figured some things out!'

She got into a rush to catch up. Sushil was still delivering pizzas. The Shangrila served Nepali food, in addition to Indian. 'There's only one other Nepali restaurant in LA, it's called Katmandu Kitchen, but it's in another part of the city—no competition,' she said. 'You want some daal-bhat, Bahini? Or—I know!' She turned to the waiter and called out, in English,

'Two orders of number five!' With Prema she switched back to Nepali. 'Can you imagine? I passed my driving licence test after three tries. I've already learned how to drive, I drive everywhere now, last week I even drove on the freeway—so fast! Like flying! We bought a second-hand car—cheap-cheap! So cheap! Everything is so cheap in this country! Our younger boy got an award at school last year. The older one's doing well too. Come to our house, it's to the south, in a place Long Beach. Where do you live? Where have you lived all this time? How have you got by?' Then she got angry all over again. 'How could you have just vanished like that?' she shouted. 'How could you just forget us? We who— Where have you been all this time?'

Prema told her, 'I fell in love with a foreigner.'

Neeru blinked, then blinked again. 'Eh.' Tentatively, she said, 'What does it matter? Nepali, foreign. We're all human beings, isn't that so? The important thing is, what is he like?'

'He is nice.'

'Sometimes I think foreigners are better than our men, they're—'

'He's half-Latino,' Prema ventured.

'Eh.' Neeru blinked again. 'That's all right,' she said. Then: 'Mexicans aren't like foreigners, they're like us: a hot blood flows in their veins. And they work very hard.' She lowered her voice: 'Can I tell you something, Bahini? I haven't hired a single Nepali in the restaurant! Only Mexicans! Our people, they work hard for Indian employers, but with one of their own they put on such airs! And how can you succeed in America if you're ashamed to work hard?'

The waiter put two plates of steaming hot dumplings before them.

'Momos!' Prema exclaimed.

'Can you believe? Momos in America!' Neeru let out a short, barking laugh. Turning to the waiter, she said, in English, 'Juan, this is my Prema-bahini. My younger sister from Nepal. She has a Mexican…' hesitatingly, 'boyfriend.'

'Hello,' Juan said.

Prema said hello.

After he left, Neeru switched back to Nepali. 'When are you getting married, then? Is the wedding date set, Bahini? What kind of ceremony? Nepali or foreign? You know, there are some Hindu priests even in America, we can get them to do all the ceremonies in the traditional way.'

Prema said, 'We're already living together.'

Neeru became grave. With some strain, she said, 'It doesn't matter, does it?' Slightly more confidently: 'It doesn't matter. Why not live together the way foreigners do? Does he cook and clean and do the laundry and dishes?'

'He does,' Prema said. 'He's—very good. But—'

'Don't be too fussy, now. I'll pray for a man like that in my next life! In this life, I'm lucky to have your Sushil-bhinaju. You'll see—he's become very modern now. He even cooks! Our boys can't believe it! But tell me, what have you been doing for work? No. Wait.' She pushed the momos towards Prema: 'First, eat.'

The momos were soft and succulent, the chicken savoury with onion, cumin and coriander. Prema felt she had never eaten anything quite so nourishing. She finished them all at one go, mumbling with her mouth full: 'Delicious.'

Neeru beamed proudly. 'I discovered wonton wrappers in the Chinese shops, and I thought: I can add momos to the menu! Eat more, Bahini. Here, I'll order another plate.'

'No, no.'

'Eat, eat.'

'No, really. Another time.'

'You know, you can come here any time,' Neeru said. 'Just come, order a plate of momos, eat, and leave. You don't even have to meet me. In America nobody has any free time to just sit around and chat, isn't that so? I am quite busy myself. But you must come to our house sometime! In a very fancy neighbourhood! Not like this. All our neighbours are foreign! And Bahini, if you need a place to live, just remember that our home is your home. We're making an apartment on the top floor to rent out. With its own entrance! Do you know how easy it is to buy a house in this country? All you have to do is ask, the banks just throw money at you. Your Sushil-bhinaju figured out how to qualify for a home loan!'

At length, she explained the intricacies of home financing to Prema. By the time she finished it had grown late, and—regretfully—Prema had to leave.

Neeru walked her to the front door. There, she once again began to scream: 'You just forgot about us! You were like family! What a selfish girl—just disappearing!'

'I'm sorry, Neeru-didi. I won't do it again.'

'I don't believe you! I don't believe you at all! You'll leave us again—you're going to go out this door, and never come back.'

'I promise I won't.'

'You'd better not!'

'I won't.'

At the door, they hugged like Americans.

Yet Prema had still not found her next direction.

The Spectre of History

~

It was late by the time she got back to the flat. Luis was in the hallway, ironing a shirt for the following day. 'There you are,' he said amiably. 'I made a tuna-fish salad for dinner. Let me finish this shirt, then we'll eat.'

She went to the kitchen, thinking: she should tell him about her forays.

'July must have tried on, like, twenty pairs of jeans,' he said, coming in. 'I just about went out of my mind! And what did you do? Where'd you go?'

'Nowhere.'

'Nowhere?'

'Just—walking around,' she said.

'Huh.'

She changed the topic: 'The board—they have not decided about the job?'

'They'll announce it in a few weeks' time,' he said. Then: 'Hey, Prema, I haven't been much fun to be around, have I? It's not fair to burden you. I'm sorry. As soon as the board makes the announcement, I'll move on. Either way, I'll move on.'

'Do not worry,' she said.

'Yeah.'

Why not tell Luis what was going on? He was so—kind. If she explained what she was feeling, he would surely understand. He would encourage her to find her direction and help her to do so, even. They would work everything out. Isn't this what people did when they loved one another? Love was—wasn't it?—everything? If so, why did she keep seeing her mother laughing, laughing at her? Why this feeling that she had to go? Even her mother had been happy in love. And Prema did love Luis: that tangle of sweet, mute emotions. Was that not love? Was it?

How could she not know?

She was just not—normal.

Seeking some guidance, she turned, one day, to Esther. The old lady had been happily married, after all. 'Tell me about Tim,' Prema said to her. 'Were you happy together?'

Esther smiled. 'What was that, dear?'

'You and Tim. Were you happy?'

'Oh, we were delighted,' Esther cooed. 'Oysters and champagne! He liked his with lemon, I like vinegar. I prefer Eastern oysters to the Pacific varieties. The Japanese varieties can be good, but to my mind there's nothing like fresh Malpeque from Prince Edward Island.'

Prema persisted: 'How long were you married, Esther? How did you and Tim meet?'

'Are the butterflies out, dear?'

'The butterflies?'

'You know, if you tell them your wishes, they'll flutter them up to God.'

The old lady was of no help.

Perhaps there was something to be learnt, though, from the

large-print romances that Esther read. Prema flipped through a few one afternoon. All their heroines found love threatening at the start, she saw; but they eventually surrendered, and found personal growth, even liberation, in the end.

In one romance, Rihanna, a successful executive, battled her attraction to Jeff, a ruthless executive at a rival company, only to discover that he had been abandoned as a child, and that his fear of love, like hers, stemmed from early rejection. They found love. In another romance, Lara had been hurt too often to ever trust a man again, till she met Rick, a jaded-seeming rock singer who wooed her with tender ballads that he composed in secret, unknown to his family and friends, his fans, and even his manager. They too found love. In yet another romance, Marilynne, a headstrong heiress, despite her initial contempt for her poor but philosophical gardener Heath, fell in love with him after he rescued her from a malicious kidnapping. Again, love.

Was *this* how she was supposed to be?

One afternoon she went into Esther's studio and examined her paintings of women in red, green, yellow. They were like the cobalt-blue woman on the living-room mantle. Their expressions were blank, blank, blank.

It just made things more difficult that Luis was so kind. One evening, he gave her a gift: a chessboard of ebony and ivory. It had belonged to his father. 'Prema,' he said, 'all the questions you asked about Dad made me think. It must be tough, leaving one country and moving to another. All these things I take for granted...I can't even imagine— I mean, I've only ever lived in America, right? Even that, only in Cali—*southern* California.'

He looked at her with those liquid, honey-brown eyes of his. 'You know, when Tina asked for a divorce,' he said, 'or even before that, when she told me she'd fallen for that dork—I kept thinking: people just get to know each other, and run into trouble, and figure it won't work. People give up so easily.' He said, 'With us—there's probably so much I'm not getting, like there must be all these phases you're going through, adjusting to a new country. It must be hard for you, Prema. The thing is, I just want to say, let's work things out together, okay? I just—I want to be there for you, no matter what. I love you.'

He wanted her to stay. The relationship was a trap. It confused her. Love confused her. Or Luis confused her. He tempted her to think: maybe there was no problem. Or the problem lay with her, with her being—abnormal. Jagged, unmade.

All the pieces in the chess set had been carved by hand. 'You any good?' Luis asked.

'No.'

'Me neither. Dad tried to teach me, but I wasn't into it,' he said. 'So he'd play this silly game with me. Wait, let me show you.' He set up the board clean, placing the pieces at random. 'You move first,' he said. 'Move any piece.'

Prema's bishop was diagonal to his king. She moved it and ended the game.

He set up the board again, again randomly. This game lasted longer: after a short chase of Prema's king, Luis won.

They played several more of these games, one after another. The longest one lasted ten minutes. Most ended quickly. In the first few moves, the king would be exposed to a fatal attack; or a pawn would knock off a bishop, then a knight, and entrap the king. And the game would end.

It made them both laugh.

'You like that?' Luis said. 'Dad kept telling me chess was like life: you have to anticipate openings and defences, you have to manoeuvre, develop, plan. He'd play this game as a joke with me—called it anarchist chess. Said it was how most people operated, smack in the middle of life, with no tactics in play.'

Carl Reyes. Carlos Reyes-Garcia. History lingered, a spectre. Nepal was haunting her through tricks of the mind, Guatemala.

A few days later, Prema finally put her tactics in play:

She went to the library and checked the Internet for news of home.

Bracing herself for the worst.

The coverage of the day was hard to follow. Prema could not understand the events being reported, or the contexts, or the chronologies. It took effort to fit all the information together.

There was a ceasefire on back home. It had been in place awhile.

There had been an accord of some kind. She couldn't quite tell how it had come about.

The Maoists had called off their war. At some stage, the UN had got involved, as had India. A peace process had got under way. But it had been preceded by a mass uprising against the king and the army. There had been an election. The monarchy had been abolished.

The country was a republic now. The army was no longer being deployed. The political parties and the Maoists were in government provisionally, drafting a new constitution.

Prema read the news again and again, trying to grasp all the changes.

A ceasefire. An accord. A peace process.

A ceasefire. An accord. A peace process.

Trying to believe it. Trying not to think of Guatemala: how the profiteers of war could turn to organized crime.

Urging herself go further, she set up a new email account. She emailed Rajan, using phonetic Nepali in roman letters: kasto chha? How are you? Her hands shook as she pushed the send button.

Then she emailed Trailokya: kasto chha?

She was shaking all over.

Nevertheless, she urged herself to go farther.

On the way back to Esther's, she stopped by the Home Wart and bought a calling card that promised a half-hour talk time for five dollars. After helping Esther into the bath that afternoon, she picked up the phone in the living room, and called her birth village.

The telephone rang, and suddenly she was speaking to an operator in her birth village: 'Ma bideshbaata phone gardaichhu,' she said. I am calling from abroad.

She identified herself and named her father, then paused to see if he would say something—her father didn't live in the village any more, or something had happened. He had fallen ill. The war. He had died.

The operator just waited for the rest of her message.

She said, 'Could you ask him to come to the telephone office at the same time tomorrow?'

'I'll tell him his daughter will call at the same time tomorrow,' the operator said.

'Do you know—?' Prema asked, 'Is everything all right there?'

'You can talk to your father tomorrow.'

She hung up, shaking.

That evening, Luis and she made love in the wordless way that had come over them of late.

Afterwards, they lay in bed, holding each other.

Luis asked, 'Hey Prema? Is everything okay? With us, I mean?'

'Everything is all right,' she said.

'I love you,' he said.

'I love you,' she said.

But she was setting out on her trail.

The following afternoon, she called her birth village again. This time, the operator recognized her voice. He put her father on.

His voice came on, soft and gravelly, across the globe: 'Is it you, Chhori?' he said. 'Is it really you?'

There was a sputtering of static on the wires.

Prema said, 'It's really me, Ba.'

The sputtering amplified over a pause.

'Are you—are you in good health, Chhori?' he asked.

'I am all right, Ba. You?'

'I am in good health,' he said. 'Chhori? It's really you? So much— Have you been well all these years? So much has happened since you left.'

'Tell me,' Prema said.

And he did:

Her sister Bijaya had come home after the ceasefire. She had spent the war years travelling from village to village, finding new recruits for the Party. After the ceasefire, she had married a member of the rebel militia, and then had a baby, a boy. She had returned to the village for his help in raising the boy. 'We are all living together here,' he said. 'Not our son-in-law, we don't know where he is, but— Your sister is safe. I am well,' her father said. 'By your mother's blessing everything is all right here.' Then he said, 'It's been an aeon, Daughter. It's safe to come back now. Nobody knows how long the peace will—'

There was a sudden choking sound, and the line went dead.

'Ba? Ba!'

In Esther's living room, Prema broke down and cried.

When she recovered, she called back, and the operator again put her father on.

She told him that she had been working, all these years, at different-different jobs in America. She told him she was presently taking care of an old lady. 'They pay well for that kind of work here,' she explained.

She did not think he would be proud of her, but he was: 'By your mother's blessings you have progressed. You have crossed the seven seas, and you have progressed, as I knew you would.'

'I can send money,' Prema said.

'No need, Chhori, no need.' He said, 'I know what it's like there. One of our neighbours—do you remember Jetha-dai? With the house across the bamboo grove? His son went to America. He's an engineer, but he works in a petrol pump in America, maybe you've met him? Jetha-dai says it's very expensive just to get by there, even rent, even food is so expensive. I understand, Chhori.'

'I can send money,' she insisted.

There was an extended pause as her father's pride battled

against his need. 'Only if you have any to spare,' he said, at last. 'Your sister— She talks about big-big things, about revolution, but with the baby it's— It's become quite hard here.'

At this, the phone card ran out of money, and the line went dead.

That evening, Luis and Prema played several games of anarchist chess, all ending in a snarl.

The next afternoon, at the library, Prema checked her email.

Both Rajan and Trailokya had replied: phonetic Nepali in roman script. Kasto chha?

She opened Trailokya's email first.

His tone was mercifully upbeat.

He wrote that he had worked in the hill bazaar till two years ago. Then the British corporation had cut off their funding, and the conservation programme had ended. Now he worked in an organization in the capital. He didn't like the work very much, but his son was going to a good private school. He wrote: 'Do you remember him? He had just started to crawl when you left. He talks all the time now! I can't get him to stop talking! So, what is it like in America?' He wrote: 'What kind of work have you found there? Are you saving American trees?'

She took in a deep breath, then opened Rajan's email.

Phonetic Nepali in roman script. Kasto chha?

Rajan had quit the organization the same year as Prema. He had teamed up with his lawyer friend in the town at the base of the hills, and launched a human rights organization there. During the war, he had headed a team of researchers, investigating human rights violations and pressuring both sides—the army and the Maoist rebels—to observe the rules of engagement. Now that the war had ended, his organization was lobbying for the prosecution of wartime atrocities. They had not got very far, he wrote. Now that there was peace, none of the political parties was keen on pursuing human rights. But he was trying. He found the work fulfilling, he wrote, but he was poorer now.

'Have you married an American?' In the next paragraph, he wrote he had got married last year. His wife was a political activist named Kalpana Bhattarai. She was well known locally, he wrote. 'Do you know of her?' She was in the political party of which Rajan had once been a member.

Prema read Rajan's message several times, then wrote back, phonetic Nepali in roman script:

Kanchhalai ke bhayo? What happened to Kanchha?

Bhetiyo? Has he been found?

She checked her email every day that week, but there was no reply. On Friday, she emailed Rajan again: Kanchhalai ke bhayo? Bhetiyo?

You Must Not Despair

~

That weekend, Luis and she argued. They had accepted a brunch invitation from Steve and Camilla; but Prema wanted to wire-transfer money to her father's account. 'You go to Steve and Camilla's. I will not go,' she said.

'Oh.' Luis said, 'Are you not feeling well?'

'I am fine.'

'You—' He said, 'You just don't want to come?'

'I have something to do.'

Luis looked at her with a hard expression she had never seen on him. 'Yeah? What do you have to do?'

She told him honestly: 'I have to send money to my father.'

'Oh.' He could not hide his surprise. 'Go-call?'

'I talked to him on the telephone this week.'

'Oh.' He said, 'How is Bee-jay? How are things back home? Huh. Where did you call from?'

'Esther's house.'

'Why didn't you tell me?' He searched her eyes. 'And everything's okay back there?'

'Yes.' She said, 'My sister got married and had a baby. A boy.'

'Wow. Huh. Why didn't you—' He frowned. 'Prema. Is there any—well, is anything going on? I feel like—' Then he asked, 'Did you tell Go-call about us?'

'About *us*?'

'Yeah.'

'No.'

'Why not?'

'I—' She said, 'He would be too shocked.'

'Because I'm American?'

'No. *Any* man.' She tried to explain. 'He is not so traditional, but he is also not so modern.'

Luis took this in. 'Yeah, I guess it's so different. It's just— I feel I don't know your world.' He said, 'You've never introduced me to any of your people.'

'I do not have any people,' Prema said. 'Not in America.' Then she realized this was not true: 'I told Meg and Neeru about you.'

'Meg's your old housemate, right? Who's Neeru?'

'I used to live with her and her husband Sushil, in Little Nepal.'

'Little Nepal?'

'Where I lived before we met.'

'When did you go there?'

'Last Sunday.'

Suddenly Luis hardened again. 'So that's where you were. I tried not to think, but I knew, I *knew*—' In anger, his voice lowered. 'Why are you sneaking around behind my back, Prema? You know, I *know* what's going on. I've seen this before. Tina—' His voice thickened: 'She got so distant. So busy. She was always running off. Doing errands, she said! Turned out she was fucking her guru!'

'Luis, it is not like that.'

'It better not be!' he said hotly.

'It is not.'

'What is it, then?' he said with a desperate look. 'Is it because I'm American you think I can't understand anything?' He took in a deep breath. 'There are ways, you know, to bridge our cultural differences. I mean, let's face it, we *are* really different. We're—completely different, in fact. I'm also finding it hard going some days. But you know—there are ways to work things out. One thing I always said to Tina was we should try couple counselling.'

'Pardon?'

'I'm just saying—' He sighed. 'It's really good of you to send money to your father.'

'I always used to send money, earlier. There is no income there—'

'What do you need, a Western Union or something? We can stop by one on the way to Steve and Camilla's.'

'There is one money-transfer company near the church that we went to.'

'Oh, you know,' Luis said, 'there's a lot of stuff going on downtown. They're cordoning off that part today, all the traffic reports say to avoid it.'

'But I must go there,' Prema said.

'There are plenty of other places. We can look one up—'

It was Prema's turn to harden. 'You said you want to go to my world,' she said. 'And I said you can come with me—'

Luis snapped. 'How the fuck is MacArthur Park your world?' Then he took another deep breath. 'Look, I'm trying, here, Prema. I'm really trying. This isn't easy for me either. It's like you're— You're shutting me out. This *isn't* about your being foreign. It's about— Fuck! I don't know what it's about!'

Her anger flared up. 'You do not need to take me anywhere! I will go by myself!'

'Um, Prema? You want to tell me what's going on?'

'Nothing!' she shouted. 'I want to go there! You do not! So why don't I go where I want, and you go where you want?'

'You'll do the money transfer and come from there to Steve and Camilla's?'

'If you want.'

'Don't *you* want to?'

'Steve and Camilla are your friends. They are part of your world, not my world.'

'So take me to your world!' He said, 'That's what I'm saying! You're shutting me out. When all I want is— Take me to your world!'

'I do not have a world!' Prema cried. 'I left the world I had, and do not belong in the one I am in now—your world. I do not have any place to take you, Luis. I do not have a place in the world.'

She had revealed a raw wound for which neither of them had a salve, and the exposure was bewildering. She left the flat, went out to the plaza bus stop, and took the bus downtown. On the long ride she looked out the cracked windows at the concrete barriers, the run-down houses, the abandoned lots and the palm trees.

As Luis had warned, there were diversions downtown, and the bus had to skirt the centre. It was well past lunchtime when she reached MacArthur Park. She walked through the clutter of groaning old buildings—Upper Mind Church Daily Donut Smoothie JESUS S VES Cappuccino—past Pedro's Electronics and Maria's Comida Salvadoreña, to the Money Gram Family Market.

An ageless old man ran the market. He spoke little English, but it was not hard for Prema to explain what she wanted. 'Nepal! In Asia! You es mi first Nepalese,' he exclaimed. Prema had never met an Ecuadorean either: she was not even sure where Ecuador was. He wired five hundred dollars from her account to her father's.

'Gracias,' she said.

When she stepped out of the market, she saw that the streets beyond had been cordoned off. The police were standing to one side. A crowd was gathering beyond them. People were holding up banners. Some were chanting. Chanting what? Slogans. It was a demonstration.

The old man came out to the market door. 'Protesta contra la guerra,' he explained. 'Boom-boom? La guerra? No good.'

'Iraq?' Prema asked.

He laughed: 'Iraq, Afghanistan, Haiti, Panama, Iran, Grenada, Cambodia, Republica Dominicana, Vietnam, Korea…'

For a while Prema studied the crowd.

Then she took a bus to the library by the boat harbour.

Kanchhalai ke bhayo?

Rajan had emailed back.

He wrote that he had not been to the hill bazaar recently, but he had heard, from those who had been there, that Kanchha's family had restored the cybercafe the previous year.

Kanchha had never been found, though. The habeas corpus writ filed on the boy's behalf had come to nothing. Kanchha's father had even paid off the middleman, in the end. A hundred thousand rupees. From his sources in the army, the middleman had discovered that the boy had been detained in the barracks for five months after his abduction. Kanchha had been blindfolded most of the time. That much, the middleman had ascertained. There had been reports, unverified, that the boy might have been tortured during interrogation. Then the boy had been moved: nobody knew where to.

Rajan wrote: 'It has been almost four years now. There are rumours of a mass grave in the barracks. Kanchha's father has given up hope, but my organization is pressuring the army to let forensic experts examine the barracks.'

He wrote: 'None of the political parties cares about anything but power. And Nepal has not signed the necessary charters to try war crimes internationally. But we are trying to find a way. And who knows? The boy may still be alive somewhere.'

'His file is still open,' he wrote. 'We are still working on his case. You must not despair.'

Sanctuary

~

Prema left the following weekend. She couldn't bear to tell Luis she was going. On Saturday Luis took July to the birthday party of her friend Gemma. As soon as they left the flat, Prema ordered a taxi. She threw her clothes into her suitcase, as well as the aquamarine marbles, binoculars and ammonite. She left behind the chess set. In the bathroom she looked out, a final time, over the parking lot. The habitat of cars. From the shelf she took Luis's cologne and sprayed some on her wrists: the citrus and mint that covered up the milk-like scent of his skin. She put the cologne back. Outside, the taxi honked. She stole away.

Neeru and Sushil readily took her in, installing her in a newly built flat on the top floor of their house, a spare, uncluttered flat with a transient feel. Neeru and Sushil were very good to her. Prema did not tell them that she had left her boyfriend, and, tactfully, they did not ask, though they surely guessed as much.

That night, she telephoned Luis: 'I had to go.'

'Yeah, I saw your stuff was gone. So—what?' he said. 'You're outta here? That's it? What the— Shouldn't we talk about this in person?'

'I would not like that right now.'

'Well, that's great. That's great, Prema. Thanks. Thanks a lot! Thanks, adiós, have a great life!'

She thought he would hang up, but he didn't. She listened to him breathing on the other end of the line. 'I am sorry, Luis.'

'I just think if— Where *are* you anyway?'

'With Neeru and Sushil. In Long Beach.'

'Can I come over? Can we talk this over?'

'I would not like that.'

'Yeah! Okay. Okay, I get it. Okay. Whatever you say. Jesus, you're really something, you know that? You're something else.'

He hung up.

He called back in a while. 'So, how long you going to stay there?'

'I do not know,' she said.

'Is this it? Is it over? Everything we had? It meant nothing to you? That sucks, you know that? What the hell kind of a person would just throw everything away? What the hell kind of a person—'

She hung up.

She called back. 'I am really sorry, Luis.'

He was silent for a long while.

'Well, you know where to find me,' he said.

'Bye.'

She was left to the world.

Tracing her way along her ever-directionless zigzag trail.

'It's been an aeon.'

If she lived frugally for a few months, she would be able to buy an airplane ticket back to Nepal.

But what would she do there?

What would she do here, though?
Nepal? America?
America? Nepal?
Everything felt wrong.

To seek sanctuary from her confusions, Prema began to leave home early, taking a bus as dawn broke north along the 130, past the Galleria—the mall—and then transferring, in a neighbourhood of aluminium warehouses, to the 232. It comforted her to be among strangers. Americans: 'The farmer's market on Figueroa, it's got a lot of history.' 'My contract says I can't name him.' 'Ganesh's Goods, sells Indian spices.' At a junction hemmed in, on all sides, by ragged houses no bigger than buses, she would transfer to the 115 westbound.

The bus would drop her off at the foot of the bluffs, by the wetlands. Summer had come, and the evaporation off the Arctic currents created a gloom off the coast. For a while Prema would stand by the wooden fence, near the no-entry sign, looking in at the small patch of wilderness. Taking in the pale, rippling light-and-shadow, the rattle and *check!* of a wren's call, the darting of movement at the edge of her vision. Following it to a pool by a dry, rocky stretch where an oystercatcher stood, immobile.

She began to come here early, bringing along her binoculars and field guide. Some mornings she saw marbled godwits with long, red upturned bills with black tips. Other mornings she got a glimpse of what lay within, the wounds of childhood. One particularly grey morning, Prema saw a break in the wooden fence. The grass was trampled down around the break. It was clear that people sneaked into the wetlands from there.

Making sure that no one was around to catch her trespassing,

Prema sneaked in through the break. And past a tangle of peas, she found herself on a well worn mud track. In one direction, the track led to the base of the bluffs, blocked off by sagebrush and—acacias? Hydrangeas. Vetch. In the other direction, it led to a vernal pool covered with dense, rustling cattails. She took that direction and sat by the pool.

The wetlands was teeming with life in the dawn, with jaegers, terns and skimmers—all members of the gull family. Shorebirds were returning north from their wintering grounds. Swallows raced through the sky, dipping and darting. Bees buzzed overhead, hovering from plant to plant. Now and then, Prema caught a larger movement and checked it through the binoculars. A flock of egrets wading. A kestrel flitting.

She returned there day after day, sneaking in through the break. One morning she saw a rookery—of herons?—in a distant willow tree. She watched whimbrels and plovers darting. And a hummingbird so small. She took in the snap and zoom of insects, the movement of energy and matter through life forms.

Afterwards, she would make her way up the bluff to Esther's house, stopping first by the boundary wall at LAX to watch airplanes taking off—one at a time, two at a time. Flying west over the Pacific, towards Asia.

The first time Prema returned to Meadowvale for Esther's check-up, she glanced beyond the registration desk, at Luis's office.

He wasn't there.

The second time, too, he wasn't in his office.

The next time, there was someone else at his desk. As Prema

approached, he glanced up with a smile. 'Good morning. And what can I do for you today?'

'Where can I find Luis Reyes?' Prema asked.

'What you want to do,' said the man, 'is go down the hall and hang right. You'll see an elevator. Take it to the third floor, then hang right again. All the way at the end—room three-oh-two. Head of Human Resources.'

He was gone, following the schema of his life.

While she was drifting and drifting. Not progressing. Just getting through one day after another. Surviving.

This was the life she had chosen? Apparently, yes. In any case: did it matter? Could she—someone like her—ever choose what to do? Could she really progress? She who had only ever followed a trail of chance and happenstance. Who had pegged her fortunes on a lottery.

At the wetlands, examining the external world, she was able to glimpse what lay coiled deep inside. Her deep lack of faith. What did it amount to, the choices made by one individual? When living was, itself, so precarious. All of humanity was fleeting. On landmasses aged billions of years, human society had spanned merely ten, fifteen thousand years. If there were an earthquake now? The San Andreas faultline lay below. This metropolis was as unstable as any village in Nepal. It could be destroyed in a single churning. It would not even take a cataclysm to destroy it. No seismic upheaval was needed, no inferno. Just an infection that was resistant to treatment. A mutating virus. A new strain of flu.

She closed her eyes and felt, all around, the shiny atoms—air, water, minerals—skittering and rushing, shiny, propelled by heat and light, as water, as minerals, from the soil to the plant, from the plant to the microorganism, to the herbivore, and on to the carnivore. The summer sky gleamed above. Her mind skittered and rushed with the sugars, the nucleic acids, the amino acids in the waters. All evanescent. The bacteria and blue-green algae, the protisia and sponges and trilobites, the mosses and ferns, the conifers and cycads and flowering plants, the molluscs, fishes, amphibians, worms, reptiles, insects, birds, mammals: all skittered and rushed.

In time the coast heated, the weather-beaten bluffs ripened. Wildflowers bloomed in the wetlands: delicate peas and clustered pink thrifts, spread-out lilac asters, foxtail barley, and round, bunched purple phlox. Prema breathed in the aroma of the grasses, the wind fragrant through the stems and stalks. She took in the sighing of the earth. Felt out her wounds, the relics below the adamantine deposits. Felt that ancient, familiar shivering in the marrow, and waited for it to pass. It always did pass. In the wetlands, the shiny atoms of her mind drifted apart, exposing, at her core, a yearning—a need—for conviction, which persisted. Even she. A Nepali from the high, misty hills. A nobody lost in America. A nothing. An ephemera. Even *she* needed to lead a complete life.

Could she, though?

Need she even bother to try?

The peas and thrifts wilted, the asters and foxtail barley dried, and the phlox fell off the stems, one by one. The wetlands stretched and contracted. Still, Prema waited—to see if she would turn twenty-seven, she realized. To see if, by some primitive superstition, she would not live past her mother's age. To see if she need make an effort at all.

And one summer's day she turned twenty-seven.

A Flutter of Blue

~

Not long afterwards, a complete stranger showed Prema how to stop drifting and set down roots wherever life might land her. Having spent some hours in the wetlands, Prema was making her way to Esther's house one morning. She had stopped by the chain-link fence to look at the airplanes at LAX. Seven had taken off within the span of a few minutes when a small, waiflike woman came, as if out of nowhere, and stood beside her.

The woman was dressed in a sky blue shirt and matching slacks. She had short red hair, and freckles all over her face. There was something ethereal about her. She looked like an elf.

She too stood looking past the chain-link fence—at airplanes? There was nothing else in that expanse, just an empty lot overrun with weeds.

They remained silent for a while. Another few airplanes took off.

Then the woman asked, 'You seen any up here?'

'Pardon?'

'Sometimes it's easier down by the dunes at Redondo. I saw one yesterday. I'm hoping it'll still be there, in fact.'

What was she saying? 'Pardon?' Prema said again.

'Oh, I thought you were looking for El Segundo Blues,' the woman said. She pointed at a shrub on the other side of the fence, a shrub with small pink flower-heads. 'That's coastal buckwheat, the only plant ESBs feed on. Do you know about ESBs? A butterfly on the federal endangered list. The airport took over an entire neighbourhood when it expanded, and turned it into a preserve for them.'

The lot on the other side of the chain-link fence was not so empty after all, Prema saw. Underneath the weeds were the ruins of demolished streets and houses.

A butterfly preserve. How come Prema had never known of the El Segundo Blue? 'You are a butterfly specialist?' she asked.

'A lepidopterist by passion, but a lawyer by training. I work at this non-profit, Life Corps.'

Prema felt she had to get to know her. 'I was a forester in my country, Nepal,' she blurted out. 'I worked in conservation.'

The woman turned to her, interested. 'They've done some great work in community forestry in Nepal,' she said.

'It is true!' Prema was thrilled to meet someone—an American—who knew this. 'What is Life Corps?' she asked. 'What kind of work do you do? Where? Here? In Los Angeles?'

The woman told her that Life Corps tracked the presence of pesticides in Southern California's marine life. 'There's still lots of DDT in the fish in this area, though its use was banned in seventy-two. There was a plant here, Montrose, it used to be a big dumper, now it's a Superfund site. But other companies still use DDT, and they're still using it in Mexico, so really, there's no chance.'

At this, all of Prema's musings about Los Angeles came bubbling out: 'The fish that people catch in the ocean—'

The woman crinkled her nose. 'The fish, the clams, the mussels. I stopped eating seafood when I found out. Then I learned about farming practices and had to go vegetarian. Even dairy—you can't drink milk once you know.' She shrugged. Then she cocked her head at Prema. 'A forester, huh. Maybe you'd be able to help me with something.' She pointed at a patch of tall grasses beside the coastal buckwheat. 'Are those dune grass or European beachgrass? European beachgrass are imports, growing all up and down the coast now. But I've read in some science journals that dune grass are making a comeback.'

The grasses had long sheaves and golden spikelets. 'I can look it up and tell you,' Prema said. 'Give me your number, I will telephone you.'

At this, the woman bridled. 'Thanks,' she said, 'but I've already got a girlfriend.'

What? 'Oh. I— I was not—' A lesbian. Prema blushed.

'Oh,' said the woman.

'No,' said Prema.

'I must have misunderstood.'

'Just, I will go to the library today,' Prema explained. 'I can look it up and tell you.'

'I wouldn't mind that at all,' said the woman. With a smile, she reached out to shake hands. 'I'm Fiona.'

'I am Prema.'

'Hi there, Prema.'

'Hi.'

Fiona, blind luck, coincidence, providence, fortuity, serendipity. Before parting, she told Prema that she was going to look for ESBs that weekend. 'Down in Redondo. My girlfriend's coming, and some other friends might join us too. Want to come along?'

'Yes, I would like that, really very much, please, thank you,' Prema burbled.

'I live just there.' Fiona pointed at the house next to Esther's. 'Come by on Saturday morning.'

And everything just fell into place.

The following Saturday, they set off in Fiona's battered van. Fiona's girlfriend Randa was an entomologist. A colleague from Life Corps, Thom, was also with them. He was a marine biologist.

On the drive south, Prema told Fiona that she had checked on the grasses in the butterfly preserve: 'They are dune grasses.'

Randa asked about the work she had done in Nepal.

Thinking back to the hill bazaar, Prema said, 'We tried to make people use less, though they are so poor, they already use so little. Compared to here. Compared to the cities there, even: the capital, Kathmandu. In the poorest areas people have nothing; but we were always saying: use less.'

Thom laughed: 'Whoa, we've got a Third World eco-warrior chick on our hands. What kind of work are you doing here?'

'I am working as a homecare attendant,' Prema said. Then she asked, 'How can I find work in conservation?' Realizing—of course. She had found her place. Not in America, and not in Nepal, but in the wilderness at the heart of human habitation.

The others knew a lot about conservation in Los Angeles, and they shared their knowledge generously.

'You might try the Sea Lab,' Fiona said. 'They have a nursery for native vegetation along the coast. I think they hire people just out of college, so you might be overqualified, but there are loads of other groups.'

'Sandy Bilder went trekking in Nepal last year,' said Randa. 'Somewhere near the Annapurna Base Camp. He came back all excited about some wildlife corridor. I bet he'd love to meet you.'

'What about Friends of Ballona?' said Thom.

'There's also that group, remember? Studying Bolsa Chica.'

'Yeah, they might have openings.'

'Do you have a résumé?' Fiona asked. 'Pass it on to me, I'll look it over and give you some guidance. You need to throw it around. Check all the websites for openings. And call people up. Knock on doors. Be persistent. Tell everyone—hey, I'm a Third World eco-warrior chick, you need to give me a job. Oh, and I've got a friend,' she said. 'Gary Song. Call him, tell him you know me, and ask him if he has any ideas. I'll give you his contacts.'

The beach that they drove to was pretty, the sand curving along the wide bay as in a picture postcard. Prema had assumed that they were going to a butterfly preserve in the area; but they stopped at the edge of the parking lot, past the cars, where the asphalt ended and the sand dunes began. The dunes were covered with coastal buckwheat.

They started looking, there, for El Segundo Blues.

It was easier to spot the larger, showier butterflies—the whites and sulfurs that fluttered up the dunes and through the parking lot, to vanish into the metropolis. The El Segundo Blue was tiny, difficult to spot. For a long time they waited and watched—and then they finally spotted one.

Just one.

Thom pointed it out to the others. The butterfly was not

even a thumb's width, perched on a pink flower-head, its wings clasped tightly together, exposing the underside, the ventral wings: white with black squares and a dash of orange. It quivered in the breeze but did not move on its own.

For a long time the butterfly stayed still. Then suddenly it flew, its grey-blue dorsal wings beating swiftly. All that was visible was a flutter of blue.

It landed on a nearby flower-head.

Again, for a long time, it stayed still. Then again it flew, a flutter of blue.

Around the dunes, Americans came and went, talking about the things that occupied them: 'Hey, did we forget the other cooler?' 'As long as the stocks keep dividing!' This tiny butterfly was what occupied the four of them.

Something calming, something corrective, took place that morning. Randa, who knew more about ESBs than the others, explained that they spent only four or five days as a butterfly, a week at most: 'So this one here? It's at the very end of its life,' she said.

The butterfly quivered in the breeze.

The perilous life of all creatures.

Randa explained what had gone into this butterfly's being here:

One year ago, on a late summer's day like today, a female would have lain scores of waxy eggs on a flower-head of one of these coastal buckwheat plants. A male would have then fertilized the eggs. When the eggs hatched a week later, caterpillars would have emerged, ravenous. They would have devoured the flower-heads—the petals, the seeds—their cuticles moulting over and over as they enlarged physically. Their wing patterns would have come to definition. Their bases would have sprouted veins. And in the fourth week the wings would have broken through the cuticles, complete with the characteristic black spots and a dash of orange.

When the flower-heads were consumed, the caterpillars would have dropped off the plant, burrowing underground for pupation. The hot autumn would have passed. The weather would have cooled over wintertime; the rains would have soaked the dunes. The warm spring, too, would have passed eventually. And when summertime came around again, the chrysalises would have undergone a violent metamorphosis, enlarging dramatically, and transforming, messily, from caterpillar to butterfly. They would have eventually emerged from below the ground, fully formed. Unfolding their wings, blood would have rushed through the veins, then dried, forming a delicate superstructure. Only then would the butterfly be ready for a season of flight.

'This little thing's been through all that,' Randa said.

At all the different stages of its life—egg, caterpillar, pupa, chrysalis, butterfly—it had had to elude predators—spiders and wasps—and other competitors for coastal buckwheat. Over the years much of its habitat had seen demolition and construction, sand and oil extraction. There were toxic particulates in the air—nitrogen oxide, nitric acid, ozone—from vehicles, factories and plants, the stream of airplanes overhead. The invasion of mallows, acacias, ice plants and other exotic plant species altered the composition of the dunes and choked out the native coastal buckwheat. A few years earlier, environmentalists had lobbied the city to replace the exotic plants with coastal buckwheat. This had allowed the ESB to gradually make a comeback. 'Used to be, El Segundo Blues occurred on this entire stretch of coast,' Randa said. The species had reached the brink of extinction, surviving only in two small preserves—at LAX, and at a Chevron refinery. But now they were recolonizing small patches outside the preserves, like these dunes.

There they were.

Or here was one. A tiny creature staying still for long stretches, then taking flight in a flutter of blue.

A Complete Life

~

Prema did not start looking, immediately, for a job in conservation. She did want to; but when she mentioned to Natalie that she was thinking of quitting, Natalie exploded: 'Okay, that's it. I've had it, I've got too much going on for this, I can't do this any more! I'm going to get Nana upgraded to Live-in Independence!'

And Prema immediately reversed herself. 'Never mind, Natalie. I will stay, I will stay.'

'I keep telling Dad I can't— What am I, a babysitter?' Natalie railed. 'I swear if you quit, I just can't— How many times have I told Dad? I can't stand it any more—'

And then, to Prema's surprise, she broke down and started to cry.

Horrified, Prema gave her word. 'I won't leave, Natalie. I promise.'

'I've got my own life to think about, you know.'

'I promise, Natalie. I will stay.'

When she thought it over later, she felt it was the right thing to do. It would have been unforgivable to abandon Esther. For, charmed as the old lady's life had been, what remained of it now? A house full of objects that elicited stray memories. A ration of daily experiences: a meal properly served, a bath, an occasional visit, lunches on the beach, books and television programmes. A few friends. A jet-black Bengal. A preoccupied granddaughter, an absent stepson and his wife. A Colombian house-cleaner and a Mexican gardener. A Nepali attendant whose name she could not remember.

Prema thought of her mother, lost to the high, misty hills. How oblivious she had been of her dying. She thought of everyone she had loved and then abandoned over the years, everyone she had left. Her father and sister. Rajan. Luis. And she thought: maybe the subjects of our affections can be interchangeable. Maybe we can be forgiven for one mistake by not committing another. She did her atonement by staying with Esther.

'What's— What's happening?'

'Nothing is happening, Esther.'

'What's happening?'

'Everything is all right, it really is.'

'Now let me see. Clio is the muse of history, isn't she? Polyhymnia. She's—epic poetry? Or is that Calliope? Love poetry? Thalia is comedy. Who else? Anna. No, no. She's—Santa Anna. No. Just Anna— Urania is—astrology. Have I told you about Tim's trip to the Shalimar Gardens?'

'Tell me.'

Late that autumn, as wildfires blazed on the hills around the metropolis, Esther suffered a stroke. She lay in a coma in the hospital for three days. Prema remained by her side throughout. Natalie took the final day off from work. Her father Theo flew in from the state of New Jersey just in time to say goodbye to his stepmother. He had a brisk, businesslike manner. That night he took Natalie out for dinner, and the following morning, a few hours after Esther died, he took a flight back to the state of New Jersey. The hospital sent Esther's body directly to a crematorium. All so efficient. A memorial service was scheduled for six weeks later, in a community hall near the bluffs.

The day Esther died, Natalie gave Prema a month's notice. 'I guess this means I'm going to have to let you go,' she said with a brief smile. 'Thanks for everything, Prema. You've been very professional. If you need a recommendation letter—'

'Thank you.'

'I'd be more than willing—'

'Thank you.'

It was not so easy to find a job in conservation. Prema began by following the leads she had got from Fiona and Randa and Thom, but none of those organizations had any openings. Some of the people she talked to there did refer her to other organizations, though, and slowly, slowly, she began to amass contacts. Then, one by one, she began to place calls: 'I am telephoning about any openings. I would like to apply for a job.'

She was eventually hired by a non-profit by an exit ramp which paid just over minimum wage. Her job was to teach schoolchildren about the California floral region. They came to the non-profit from inner-city schools and sat in the garden, all weeds and scrubs, that had been restored to native vegetation. They listened reluctantly, resentfully even, as Prema explained the threat that introduced plants posed to native plants, and to their consumers—insects, birds, animals. Some of the children asked smart questions. 'Isn't that, like, racist?' a boy asked one day with a sing-song accent Prema could not place. 'It's like you're saying only American plants are good and all foreign plants are bad, like those crazy Minutemen people who want to stop the Mexicans from crossing the border.'

His classmates sniggered.

It had fallen on Prema to explain to American children that preserving biodiversity wasn't just for saving insects, birds, animals. 'It is a time of mass extinction on earth. Human beings are killing many more species than nature is replacing. This is called ecological collapse. Meaning, we do not have enough to live on any more. Human beings are losing their habitat.'

The boy said, 'Are you saying *we're* going extinct?'

'Many scientists are saying yes.'

'Aw, man!'

Through the non-profit, Prema was gaining an affinity for this land, at last; though she did still find America strange. It did not have to be the way it was. But then Nepal, too, did not have to be the way it was. People everywhere were complicated, maybe. Or Prema did not understand them. She kept to what stirred her convictions: Botany. Biology. Biogeography. Through her colleagues—Nancy and Haroun, Sarah, George—she was slowly learning about the interconnections, dependencies and linkages of the natural world. The survival of the human species depended, she had learned, on the continued survival of the California floral region. Why did so few Americans know this? With her colleagues she travelled, a few times, beyond the metropolis, to the desert. She wanted to go farther, to travel from the Mexico border all the way up to the sequoia and redwood forests in the north.

She still lived in the flat in Neeru and Sushil's house. Every now and again, she met Meg at an Indian restaurant to share a vindaloo. Meg would talk and talk and talk, and sometimes pause to let her say something. Prema never did tell Meg that she was Nepali, and not Indian. Did it matter?

She also joined Neeru and Sushil when they were visiting compatriots. She befriended the couple she had met in Little Nepal—Sarala and her reedy, pleasant-faced husband—and they exchanged experiences and advice in this, their in-between existences. Prema's being single seemed to needle all her compatriots. Neeru and Sushil often volunteered, only half in jest, to arrange a marriage for her. 'It's not like it used to be, Bahini,' Neeru would say to her in confidence. 'Our boys these days don't mind if a girl has had—some attachments—before marriage.' With so many compatriots coming to America every year, Neeru told her, she should find one of her own kind.

Prema had already found her own kind: Fiona, Randa and Thom, and Nancy, Haroun, Sarah and George, and others whom she got to know through them. What did it mean to live a complete life? She was free. She was in good health. She had not got rich in America, but she had enough to eat, she had shelter and clothing. She was not affected by war or afflicted by the basis for it: overconsumption. She was content. Her life was complete.

Yet, of course, uncertainties remained.

Once a month, she went to the Money Gram Family Market to wire money to her father; and the wondering—is this really where I should be living?—always flared up. There were constant nagging questions—should I stay, should I go? Have I gone too far, or not far enough? Was this progress enough? Or should she try to progress further? Perhaps it was her fate—the fate of those like her—to always wonder. Having made a decision to live in one place, to always experience pangs of doubt whether the *other* place, or some other place altogether, wasn't the one to live in. While doing one thing, to regret not having done the other. That nagging uncertainty—never knowing, never knowing for sure, or at all—remained with her.

She had doubts, too, on other matters. Love still confused her. Or relationships confused her. Or sex did.

The first man she dated after Luis was Fiona's friend Gary Song, a PhD candidate at USC, researching the eutrophication of California's coastal estuaries. His work was so fascinating that Prema could not help being drawn to him. And though she could not help thinking of Luis when he kissed her, she slept with him: in bed he was like a gale, a fast, sweeping force.

After him there was Haroun Rahman, a colleague at work who took Prema stargazing and convinced her to go home with him afterwards. It turned out to be a mistake, as he was looking for a long-term relationship. The awkwardness between them eventually passed.

After Haroun was Bobby Sorensen, a forester originally from the state of Maine, a friend of Fiona and Randa's. Bobby had a full, feckless laugh, and he was full of stories. Prema and he slept together several times, but she stopped seeing him when he confessed that he was starting to feel a certain fondness for her.

Prema avoided getting into relationships. She went on dates; and these dates sometimes led to sex. Casual sex. And that was that. For she felt no sweet, mute emotion with these men. Or she would not allow it to develop. If the biological purpose of sex was to foster love, and marriage, so as to aid with child-rearing, she did not need a relationship, because she did not want to be married or to have children. Her desires were manageable if she stopped seeing a man after a few dates.

After Bobby, Prema dated José Marco, a schoolteacher who came with his students to the non-profit. He did not call her after their first date and she did not mind. After José she dated Simon Conway, though they only held hands, and never had sex. So. The relationship she had got into with Luis: it had been a mistake. Someone as jagged and unmade as she: how could she fit into the format of a relationship, American or Nepali?

Yet of course she wondered.

The Man Who Kept Reappearing

~

She wondered especially because she kept seeing Luis, a phantom of lost love. He kept reappearing to haunt her.

The first time, she saw him at Esther's memorial service, six weeks after her death. The community hall was not far from the Home Wart. When Prema got there, Natalie was at the door, greeting visitors: 'Wonderful that you could make it.' Her father Theo and Theo's wife Mary were also there: 'Thank you so much for coming. Please go in. The service will begin soon.'

Inside, the hall was surprisingly crowded. Prema took a seat near the middle of the hall. Sam was sitting in the first row, beside Elizabeth Beard and Donald Alden. Mercury was in the hall, as was Romiro. They nodded at each other. Prema did not recognize anyone else. Were these the people whose names had been on the kitchen corkboard: Randy Miller, Jen Rustig, Morgan Hausman, Jay Kleeberg, Beth Martis, Danny Brenson?

In a while, a pastor—Elizabeth Beard's husband—stood on a dais and recited a prayer. Then Theo and Natalie took turns to speak about Esther. Next, an art dealer effused over Esther's paintings. Prema learnt that Esther had been quite famous. She had been part of a well known art group from the 1970s whose members painted in a self-consciously feminine style. Her paintings were in museums and private collections all over the world. After the art dealer finished talking, someone read a poem. Someone sang. Then the pastor recited another prayer.

It was a thoughtful service. It gave everyone a chance to acknowledge: Esther King had been in this world, and now she was gone. Prema was moved by it.

It was when she got up to leave that she saw Luis. He had taken a seat at the back, and—she could not tell if he had seen her—was already leaving the hall when she saw him. She did not try to catch his attention. Instead, she lingered. She let him go.

A year later, she saw Luis again, this time in transit at the Bangkok airport. In a sparkling-white hall, Prema was going one way on the moving walkway, and Luis was going the other way, pushing a luggage cart. By the time Prema registered his face—by the time she named him in her mind, told herself she was mistaken, and looked back to check—he had got off at the far end, and was turning into a side hall. She stopped herself from turning back to make sure it was him: it could not have been him. She had made a mistake.

The flight from Bangkok passed uneventfully, the hours stretching over the dateline. When she had made the reverse journey, five years earlier, she had looked out at the sky. She did the same this time.

She was returning from a visit to her birth village. Centuries away. It was the first time she had been back since leaving home at the age of seventeen. To get to her birth village, she had to take a bus from the capital, and after a day-long ride, stay overnight at a highway town. The following morning she set out early on a seven-hour trek.

Centuries.

The footpath wound higher and higher through the hills, past sleepy, forgotten villages and fields ripening, in the autumn, with rice. Every now and then, the mountains would be visible through the lowering mist. She glimpsed Mount Everest through the clouds on a ridge.

The air grew cool and moist as she entered her village. There were a few new buildings near the front, but her family house—sturdy, two-storeyed, of stone—was as she remembered it, if smaller, more cramped in proportion to her adult body. The bamboo grove, the Shiva-Parvati temple, the terraced rice fields were little altered. The village was covered in mist. Prema shivered throughout her visit.

Her father was overjoyed to see her. 'By your mother's blessings you have crossed the seven seas, and you have returned,' he said, greeting her with a teeka of red powder and a marigold garland. 'I didn't think I'd live to see this day.' He was very aged, but still spry. He looked at her proudly through milky eyes. His grandson, already toddling, was clutching his legs. Prema's nephew: Bijaya's son.

Bijaya was standing at the threshold, staring on at the reunion. She was tall now, taller than Prema, with a sturdy build, but with the same taciturn, mulish air she had had as a girl. She smiled briefly when Prema acknowledged her, then returned to staring as their father led Prema in, fussing over her.

'You've grown so,' Prema said to her sister.

Bijaya laughed. 'Wouldn't I have? After all these years.' She turned away to attend to her chores.

Prema instantly recoiled. She remembered what Bijaya had said to her as a girl: 'I hate where we're from.' Did she blame Prema for abandoning her?

Over the days, Prema met her relatives, neighbours, family friends. There was a small hubbub in their house. Otherwise, the village was moribund. There was a punishing drudgery to life here. Most of the young people had left for the cities. A few had joined the Maoists. Others had gone abroad in search of jobs. A neighbour, Jetha-dai—whose son worked in a petrol pump in America—was readying to send another son to work in a construction company in Dubai. Other neighbours had family members—mostly sons, but a few daughters, too—in Korea, Malaysia, Japan. A distant cousin of Prema's had found work as a gardener for an Arab sheikh in Kuwait. One of the most promising village boys had become a guard for an American security contractor in Iraq. Family members in the village were sustained by the earnings of those gone abroad.

Prema kept trying to talk to Bijaya; but though her sister would answer questions, she would not be drawn into conversation.

'Your son looks just like you did as a child.'

'It's natural, isn't it?'

'Is there anything I can do around the house?'

'What's there to do?'

'I can help.'

'There's nothing to do.'

Was there accusation in this? Rebuff? Or something else? Judgement? Did she think of Prema politically—as a class enemy? Prema found herself judging Bijaya in turn. A former Maoist? A Maoist.

The idiot girl.

Prema did not ask, and Bijaya did not tell her, about what she had done during the war. Nor did Bijaya talk about her husband, other than to mention, once, that he was off working for revolution by peaceful means. Their father seemed to think he had left her for good, but Bijaya clearly thought otherwise. The idiot, idiot girl. *This* was the future she had seen for herself?

'I hate where we're from.'

In the evenings, as Bijaya cooked dinner for the family, their father would ask Prema about her life in America. She would tell him about the work she had done over the years, and about the work she was doing now. From the wood stove Bijaya would stare at her. Prema felt such rejection from her. It made her so angry. Though she tried to reason with herself: Bijaya would at least be in the village for their father as he aged…whereas she, she would be centuries away.

Not far enough.

The morning she was to leave, she sat in the bamboo grove listening to the susurration of the wind.

Some wounds stay raw, perhaps. After taking leave of her father, and kissing her nephew goodbye, Prema turned to her sister, standing by the threshold of the house.

'I'm leaving, Bahini.'

'Go well,' she said.

'I don't know when I'll be back,' Prema said. 'But I'll try.'

Bijaya nodded tersely.

Prema needed more than that, though. She took her sister's hand, and lowering her voice, said, 'You know, Bahini, you were right, all those years ago. When I last left. You said I wouldn't come—and you were right. Do you remember? We talked by the bamboo grove? You said you hated where we were from. And—'

Bijaya stiffened. 'Why would I ever say something like that?'

'You were just a child,' Prema said. 'But you were right. That's how I felt, too. I also—'

'But I love my country.' Bijaya's eyes glittered fiercely. 'Everything I've done—I do—is for my country, for the liberation of my country, my people. How can anyone hate where they're from?' she said, spitting out her words. 'It's like hating your mother,' she said.

Stunned, Prema turned to the footpath leading out of the village, desperate to be gone.

And yet, as her birth village receded into the mists, a sharp grief stabbed through her. Should she really be leaving?

A few hours down the footpath, she fell in with a foreigner, a man with long, shaggy hair, who was working as a consultant at a non-government organization. They got talking. Sergio De Fazio was from Peru. At first he spoke to Prema in slow, broken Nepali. When she switched to English, he gratefully followed. A garrulous man, he talked about the war in his own land, the atrocities committed, the suffering of ordinary people. 'It is not so bad here, it's bad, but not so bad—thank god.' Sergio had full, brown lips and a wide smile. He distracted Prema from her confusions. Nearing town, they realized they were staying overnight in the same lodge. At dinner—freshly showered, and feeling lighter of spirit—Prema watched him drink too much whisky. Her being Nepali seemed to make him nervous. After dinner, he invited her to his room, but seemed to worry that she might be a prostitute, or that a local romance would complicate his life. She could see the questions in his eyes. This did not keep them from having sex. Prema returned to her room at midnight, and the next morning paid the bills and boarded her bus before Sergio had woken up.

Landing in Los Angeles this time, she recognized the watery curve of the bay, the dark, silhouetted hills, the broken grids of the metropolis.

What was she doing here?

She was waiting by the luggage carousel when she saw Luis again. He was at the far side of the hall, at another carousel, waiting for his luggage from another flight. This time Luis—surely just a man who looked like him—was facing in her direction, but he was far enough away so that she could not be certain it was him. She wanted to be sure. Leaving the carousel, she weaved through the throngs of waiting passengers, reaching him just as he stooped to lift a blue suitcase. The man looked up, a stranger, and saw her staring at him, and gave her a puzzled smile. She shook her head to say: Nothing. He turned away. A phantom.

Bastard Love

~

Then she saw him again a week later. She had gone to the beach to look, once again, for the El Segundo Blue, a summertime ritual now. She was standing at the edge of the lot examining the coastal buckwheat when a girl walked by. July: taller than she used to be, and with short, spiky hair. She was with a friend. Gemma. And behind them, Luis.

Luis saw Prema too, and stopped.

His liquid, honey-brown eyes.

She stared at him, and he stared at her, and for a while neither found anything to say.

Then: 'Prema.'

'Luis.'

'Hey.'

'Hi.'

'Hi there.'

'Hello.'

The girls walked on, absorbed in their own conversation.

'You—' Luis said, 'How you doing?'

'All right.'

'God,' he said.

'You?' she asked.

'Good. Great.' He nodded. 'I'm doing great,' he said. Then, 'How— What— Where are you, these days?'

'With Neeru and Sushil. Those are the people—'

'Yeah, I remember the names. Long Beach, right? Yeah. Good. Great.'

July and Gemma had stopped by the sand, waiting for him.

'Guess I should go,' he said.

'All right.'

'Bye, Prema.'

'Bye.'

'But it was good to see you,' he said.

'Yes.'

'God.'

'Yes.'

He didn't go. Instead, he said, 'Hey, want to get together sometime? Not to— We never really got a chance to talk things over, you know? Think we could try now? It's just— I never really understood what happened.'

'I am free on Friday evening,' she said.

'Dinner? Sure. Hey, Long Beach isn't that far, I could pick you up after work and go somewhere.'

'Shall we go to the beach near Esther's house? I have not been there since she died.'

'You know, I saw you at her service but I was too bummed out to talk.'

'I saw you also.'

'Yeah. So, Friday, huh.'

She gave him her address and telephone number.

He showed up right on time on Friday evening. Prema answered the door, and asked him in to the living room, where Neeru and

Sushil were pretending not to be lingering around in the hope of meeting him. Prema made the introductions: 'Luis, meet my Neeru-didi and Sushil-bhinaju.'

Neeru greeted him with a very firm handshake. '¡Hola, Luis! ¡Bienvenido! ¿Cómo estás?'

'A very great pleasure to make your good acquaintance,' Sushil said with extreme formality.

Luis, for his part, came out with: 'Nah-mass-tay Neeru-dee-dee, Soo-sheel-been-a-jew.'

Then there was a pause, a pause motivated, apparently, by everyone's desire to do nothing socially incorrect.

Finally, Sushil asked: 'Can I get you a coffee?'

Prema intervened. 'We will be late, Bhinaju.'

Luis agreed: 'The freeways will be jammed if we don't get moving.'

Sushil shook his head agreeably. 'La ta.'

'Very nice to meet you both,' Luis said, shaking hands with them again.

'Go well,' Sushil said.

Neeru: 'Adiós.'

Outside, Prema burst out laughing: 'I forgot, Neeru thinks you are Mexican.'

'You told them I'm Mexican?'

'I told her you are half-Latino, and she understood it like that.'

He laughed. 'Yeah, funny how that happens.'

He led her to a blue car with silver trimmings and a smart shape. A new car.

'A Civic?' she asked.

'A Prius.' He opened the doors. 'Know how hard it is to get one of these babies? They're all sold out, even for second-hand there are waiting lists. There was this guy at Steve's radio station who wanted to sell it—and I swooped right in. Know what a Prius is?'

'A hybrid.'

'Low emissions, high efficiency, the works. Hey. How come you knew that?'

She smiled. 'Even I know some things about cars.'

She had brought a present for him. She now held it out to him.

'What is it?'

A *Rough Guide to Nepal*. She said, 'You showed me America. This is if you want me to show you Nepal one day.'

He stared at it a bit oddly. 'Thanks,' he said. 'Cool. Thanks. Thanks.' Then he cleared a spot for it in the back seat, in between the T-shirt, baseball cap, running shoes and flip-flops.

As they drove, Prema told him about Esther's last months. 'I knew she was going, but when it happened—' She said, 'I did not notice when my mother died, I was too young. Just—one day she was gone. With Esther I wanted to be there all the way. But maybe it is always sudden. One day the person is just not there.'

'Yeah—what it was like with Dad.'

'You got the job,' she said. 'Head of Human Resources.'

'Yeah.' He laughed, 'I get to do even more paperwork now!'

Past the freeway, he turned past the skyscrapers by the high-tension wires to the traffic lights at the underpass. From there, he turned on to the wetlands. Past the Home Wart, he parked by Esther's house—or what used to be her house. Did Natalie still live there? They got out and walked along the chain-link fence towards the beach.

Prema pointed at the expanse beyond the fence. 'Did you know that is a butterfly preserve?'

'Yeah. For the El Segundo Blue.'

'Why did you not tell me?' she asked. Then she answered herself: 'Because we did not know what each other knew and did not know.'

'Say that again!'

'I was looking for El Segundo Blues at the beach when we met.'

'What's that called: butterfly-watching?'

'Butterflying. When we saw it, it was—cool,' she said. 'This small!' She held up a digit of her thumb. 'Grey-blue on the top, and white and black and orange on the bottom. When it flies it looks so—cool.'

At the beach, they walked along the sand to the pier laid on top of the massive drainpipe. The sun was lowering on to the horizon, the sky was ablaze. They watched the sun set. Then Prema told Luis about the work she was doing. 'It is like the work I was doing in Nepal, but better, because I am working with Americans, who are really a big problem for the environment. My work makes more of a difference—globally, I mean.'

'Sounds like you're doing real well.'

'I just came back from my birth village,' she said.

'Whoa. How's your family?' he asked. 'Go-call and Bee-jay?'

'They are all right. My sister had gone away for many years, now she is back with my father. She and her son.' Prema wondered whether to tell him she had been, was still, a Maoist;

but she left it at that. 'You?' she asked, 'What is happening with you?'

'Me? Well, I—' He patted his belly. 'I got into a gym routine. Four times a week.'

She let this evasion pass. 'You look good.'

'I'm older, too—thirty-six! Over the hill!'

After the last of the sun disappeared below the horizon, they walked north, towards the bridge over the cement-lined creek. Many people were out on the bridge that evening: scores of lone fishermen, and groups, and some entire families standing by rows of fishing poles. One man had just reeled in a fish. It was twitching on the line. Luis asked the man what kind of fish it was. 'Tuna,' the man replied. 'Yellowfin.' He unhooked it and put it in a cooler, where it thrashed and twitched, asphyxiating.

Farther along, they passed a woman casting a line. Nearby, two children were huddled in blankets, watching cartoons on a portable DVD player. Their father was stooping over his rod, waiting for a bite.

They stopped at the far end of the bridge. The dusk was deepening. The stars were showing, though faintly. Prema pointed out a few constellations to Luis. Orion, to the west. Ursa Minor, farther north.

'Cool.'

She caught a whiff of citrus and mint in his movements. And felt the stirrings of a sweet, mute emotion.

Then they went to a harbour-side diner, and talked.

'How is July?' Prema asked. 'I am sorry if I made things difficult for her by leaving.'

'She's good, she's good,' Luis said. 'When we broke up, she

said, "Dad, did you get dumped?" That's what she said. She said, "Dad, you got dumped!"' He laughed. 'She doesn't miss a trick, July. It gave her a chance to give me relationship advice—oh, she loved that part! You know, she's gone punk now,' he said. 'Or post-punk. Whatever. We're arguing about whether she can get body piercings.'

'So: new job and new car. You have a new flat too?' she asked.

'Flat.' He laughed. 'I was thinking of making a bid for this condo in Manhattan Beach, but I didn't. I figured—' He looked away, then said, 'I don't really need a bigger place if it's just me, so I splurged on the Prius instead. I— I—' He said, 'Turned out to be lucky I didn't go for the condo, with the recession and all. But the Prius, I— It wasn't like I knew if we'd ever talk again, Prema, but I thought—if you knew I had bought a hybrid, you'd be proud of me.'

Outside the window, Prema heard the flap of some shorebirds she could not see. An insect buzzed by in the dark.

He said, 'You left a real mark on me, Prema.'

'I am sorry I hurt you.'

'No, I mean you changed me.'

'But I also hurt you. Luis,' she said, 'I think I am not normal, I am— I am a little bit screwed.'

'Screwed-up, you mean. No, well, you've been through a lot. I should have seen that, I should have been more sensitive.'

'No, it was my fault. You were very kind to me.'

'*Kind*?' He laughed. 'I wasn't being *kind*, Prema. I was— I *loved* you. I was thinking we'd get married, you know? I was thinking that we'd work everything out.' He said, 'I made such a mess of my first marriage I wanted to do it right this time. I was even thinking you'd want a kid, I was psyching myself up for another brat—'

'Brat?'

'A child.'

'No children,' Prema said.

'No children?' Luis said.

'No children,' she said.

'Like, never?' he said.

'I don't think so.'

'But kids are— It's amazing, having a kid. You know, the greatest thing I ever did was have July.'

'I have never wanted to have children. Having children is—dangerous,' Prema said. 'And there are too many human beings already on the earth. It is not good for the environment.'

He stared at her. Then: 'I guess because of your mom—Though it's not really dangerous if you have proper health care. I mean, the hospitals in America are pretty good—' Then he caught himself. 'Anyway, I'm just saying.'

They were silent awhile.

Then he changed the subject. 'Hey, you want to hear something stupid I did?'

After she left him he had gone to Tina, convinced that she was unhappy in her marriage with Christopher. He tried to get her back. Tina refused; but they finally got a chance to talk through everything that had happened between them. 'I asked her why she left me, I mean why *really.* And why women leave me, what am I, like, not good enough—?' He laughed. 'You know what? She looked at me like I was such a sucker. She said I'm, like, a girl. I always need someone, I feel like I'm no one if I'm not in a relationship. And I realized—what's wrong with that, you know?' He shrugged. 'Okay, so does that make me a—wuss? I'm mean, I've dated a bit since— There was this one girl. But I want something meaningful,' he said. 'For me it's like—people make up our lives, you know. Right? There's only people, that's all there is. I— What about you?' he asked. 'You seeing anyone?'

'No.'

'No?'

'Not right now.'

There was another silence.

He said, 'Well it's too bad we never had kids, 'cause they would have been pretty damn all-American: half-Nepali, a quarter WASP, a quarter Guatemalan.'

She laughed.

He laughed.

And a flash of something—affection—passed between them. She instinctively retreated; but he pursued that emotion. He said, 'I mean, just because it was hard didn't mean it wouldn't work. We gave up so easily—'

'Luis.'

'Yeah. Okay. I know,' he said. 'I mean, it wasn't easy for me either. It was real hard after you left, my confidence really went into a tailspin. I'm not even sure I want to try again. But it must have been worse for you, with all the stuff you were going through. I understand.'

Did he?

Did she?

'You know how else you changed me?' he said. 'I found this group that helps refugees from Central America, and I gave them some money.'

'Is it El Rescate?'

'How do *you* know them?' he said. 'All those things you were telling me about the war reminded me about how lucky I am. And it's—gratifying—to be able to give. Plus the donations are tax-deductible.'

Afterwards, they walked back along the bridge. Night had fallen. The family who were out fishing were still there. The man who had caught the yellowfin tuna had caught two more fish. They lay gleaming in a bucket. Sea bass.

'Nice catch,' Luis said to the man.

'Best I ever had,' the man replied.

'Good going, man.'

'You folks have a nice night now.'

When they were out of his earshot, Prema told Luis about the DDT in the marine wildlife.

'Jesus.' He shuddered. 'It all looks so innocent, doesn't it? People out fishing. But when you think about it— God.'

They walked back along the chain-link fence to Luis's car, and then he drove Prema back home, parking outside Neeru and Sushil's house.

'Hey, thanks,' he said, of the *Rough Guide* on the back seat. 'And thanks for—meeting. I really enjoyed that. And it was really good to talk.'

'For me too,' she said.

'You going to be okay?'

'Yes. You?'

'I guess. Yeah.'

He leaned in and kissed her on the cheek.

She caught the citrus and mint of his cologne. And underneath the cologne: the scent of milk.

Bastard love.

Luis said, 'I really loved you, Prema.'

She said, 'I loved you too, Luis.'

They looked at each other. They knew what the other was thinking.

He said it first: 'Think we could meet again? I don't— You think we could go out again? Not to— Just on a couple of dates, see how things go? You think we could?'

'Do you think?' she said.

'Dunno.'

'I don't know too. I really am a bit screwed.'

'We're all screwed,' he said. 'So what do you think?'

'What do you think?' she said.

They kept looking at each other.

Yes?

No?

Yes?

No?

She took a chance on the lottery, the lottery of life.

'Yes,' she said.

Acknowledgements

~

I owe a great debt to Ravi Singh, who has nurtured my writing and been the generous and insightful and also plainspoken editor that all writers dream of. Many thanks to him, Paromita Mohanchandra and the stellar team at Penguin India, who first published this book. I would like to thank Aleph for reissuing it so attractively. My thanks also to Bruce Westwood and Carolyn Forde in Toronto for helping me complete this novel with conviction. I began the first draft during intensely shaky times in Nepal. My profound thanks to Khushwant Singh, Madhu Sarin, Gurcharan and Bunu Das, Urvashi Butalia, Bharat Bhushan, Sheela Reddy and Jaya Bhattacharji Rose for helping me find stability in Delhi. I am also grateful to Wayne, Judy and Rachel Amtzis, Kesang Tseten and Barbara Weyermann, and Mea Arnold in Kathmandu; Maya Sonenberg and Shawn Wong in Seattle; Kari Karanko in Helsinki; and John Bevan, Elana Dallas and Alastair Hatchett in London, who have, in very different ways, helped me to keep writing. Mandira Sharma's brave work in human rights has informed my depiction of the war in Nepal. Catherine Rich and Travis Longcore of Urban Wildlands very generously shared their passion for and knowledge of conservation in Los Angeles, and showed me the